Twisted Love

Charmaine Williamson

First Edition

NEWMAN SPRINGS PUBLISHING
320 Broad Street
Red Bank, NJ 07701

First originally published by Newman Springs Publishing 2019

ISBN 978-1-64096-952-0 (Paperback)
ISBN 978-1-64096-953-7 (Digital)

Printed in the United States of America

I want to thank myself for the hard work and dedication
I've put into this project and my support system
that's been with me every step of the way!!
Note to SELF... Take More Chances C.A.N...

As the equipment went down one by one, Felicia refused to give in and stress out. She put her headphones on and blasted her music, stepping out into the cold world of Ohio. It was the middle of April, and they were still experiencing winter temperatures. She hit one machine at a time jamming and thinking on her next move. She loved the airport, but after ten years she felt she'd had enough of the place. The drama was becoming unbearable with the elderly women along with the fair shared deaths around the place.

She headed to the last machine to load the last box of tickets, when she caught a glimpse of the sky. Emerald colors reigned across the atmosphere, and the moon burned bright. The scenery spoke to her. She felt it deep in her soul that this was her time. She returned to the office in hopes that would be the last time she had to leave out for the day.

She sat in the office away from everyone still listening to the music ring through her headphones. She began to think about Derek and how'd he been over the last few years. The last time they spoke, things had gotten so far out of hand with the arguments and mania matches because of the constant lies he told. She didn't understand the life he chose to live, and he could care less about how she wanted to live hers, but that was the man she had fell for. She loved everything physically about this man, from his smooth chocolate skin to his soft eyes that told a story way deeper than the cold exterior he wore on the outside. They were from two totally different sides of the track. Even with logical thinking she fell for him hard.

Sitting there in deep thought, she wondered if she had crossed his mind after all these years. Her conscience was telling her she missed him, but she refused to be the first one to give in. In every argument they had, he could always find a way to switch that shit around on her and have her all fucked up. She should have listened when the twisted bastard told her he wasn't the lovable type, but she had to face it. She was still deeply intrigued by him. The office phone rang and startled her back to reality. She listened to the cashier give instructions, and that's when it hit her. *Damn! I forgot to hit my planks this morning.* She could feel the bitterness building, but it had to be done.

The day seemed like it was taking forever to end from her point of view, but everyone in the office was enjoying their evening while she sat there wondering if she really wanted to do a full-body workout tonight or just focus on her arms and back. "Damn! How the hell did I forget about my ab workout?" Felicia stated to herself.

Surfing the net Felicia happened to scroll past a very familiar name. Her heart fluttered once her eyes studied the profile picture. "What the *fuck*! *Derek*!" She glared at his picture for a few seconds letting it sink in. She was just thinking about him, and here he was. *Bing!* The notifications lit up. Derek was asking to be friends after all these years. *What type of sick joke is the universe playing right now?* Felicia thought to herself. She accepted the friend request, and shortly after her DM was going crazy with "How have you been?" and "How long it's been since we last spoke back in 2012?"

It was now 2020, and Felicia was married, not so much happily but good enough for today's society. Felicia decided to answer all the questions that Derek was asking. Waiting until the perfect time, she slipped a question of her own in on him. It had been years, and now all of a sudden, he wanted to hit her up. "Where have you been, Derek?" Felicia came on out with it boldly. Patiently waiting on a response, her mind began to wander to the last encounter they had, him standing in the middle of her living room with his pants down begging for a blow job and her refusing as she laughed at him.

Derek began to explain that he had been in prison for some trouble he had gotten into a few years back. Felicia heard the rumors he was accused of, but she wasn't the type of person to believe everything that someone else told her; however, his confirmation to the stories she heard was like a gut punch. He was a full-blown criminal or pedophile. A part of her always knew that one day he would get himself into something stupid, but to be involved with a seventeen-year-old girl was mind-boggling for Felicia.

After the ice was broken, Derek saw his chance to find out a little piece of Felicia's life. He began to ask about her schedule, and without hesitation she gave it to him so trusting. Going into details from morning to night, she told him rituals, but it was the gym that sparked his interest once it was mentioned; however, her hours of going snagged his plans. He had a limited amount of time out before he had to return back to the halfway house for curfew. When he explained everything about his curfew to Felicia, she felt sort of a relief because she was in no hurry to see him.

Felicia's mind drifted off again to another moment with her and Derek—the way they used to make love to one another and the way his body would always be in sync with hers. She loved the aggression he applied when he was intimate with her. He was everything she had been craving, and now he was back. Felicia's phone buzzed several times bringing her back to reality once more. Derek was confessing how he was still in love with her after all these years and how he would do anything to get her back. Once Felicia stopped responding the messages went cold quickly. After a few minutes to clear her mind of the thoughts she was just flirting with, Felicia decided to respond by telling him if they were going to continue the conversation, it couldn't be about the past. He was clearly trying to rekindle something Felicia thought, and she wasn't feeling it although her body felt otherwise.

Derek didn't like the sound of things already, so he started throwing information at her about her husband, letting her know that he knew exactly whom she was married to and where he worked.

He went on to tell Felicia about certain stuff that she hadn't even told him about her husband. Feeling concerned Felicia immediately stopped texting and called Derek's phone. She had to know how he knew the shit he was spouting out his mouth. Answering the phone Derek chuckled.

"What are you calling me for, boo? I didn't scare you, did I?" he asked with a sarcastic tone.

"You're a fucking psycho, dude! You really have been stalking my husband?" Felicia replied.

"I haven't been stalking shit, baby. I got eyes on the streets, and they see things. It's that simple," he said calmly.

"Well, it's still considered stalking, you freak, if people are reporting information that you're requesting. Let's just let bygones be. We don't need to try to rekindle anything. I'm married! You've been in prison. We finally got each other out of our system, so we can go on with our lives. Do you feel me?" Felicia spoke with such sincerity in her voice. However for her, Derek didn't give two shits about any of the shit she had just said. She could feel from how dead-end the conversation went that Derek wasn't paying her any mind, and she was starting to feel like a dumbass for telling him her schedule now. Derek had finally reached an all-time low with Felicia. She was now freaked the fuck out and wanted nothing more to do with him. With nothing left to say, she ended the phone call as polite as possible.

Sitting at her desk Felicia couldn't believe the shit that just took place. How fucking long had this fool been out of prison to find out all this bullshit about her and her husband? Felicia felt nervous in her stomach about the conversation. She knew Derek and the shit he was capable of back in the day. Nobody ever crossed Derek, and everybody who was somebody knew whatever Derek wanted he could have it whether it be given or taken. "I must have been full-blown stupid to mess with a fucking thug. Now I'm scared about it," Felicia stated to herself as she chuckled the fear out of her system.

The clock struck 11:00 p.m., and Felicia was already at the time clock swiping her badge. She headed toward the door when her phone buzzed again. It was one last message from Derek telling her that he would always be in love with her. She was his soul mate who got away. Derek demanded that she give their love another shot! Felicia read the message, but she made her mind up about not conversing with Derek anymore. She hit the power button and shut the screen down as she got into her car and headed home to her family.

Arriving home Felicia had just enough time to freshen up and get dressed while her cousin Jon rolled a blunt. Back out the door with her cousins Jon and Jay C, she went not uttering a word to her husband about her day nor the past that sprang back up.

Pulling up at the gym, Felicia and Jon finished the rest of their Mary Jane, while Jay C headed inside for his ordinary night of work. As Felicia followed, Jon took his last few hits and headed into the gym two minutes off her tail. The boys hit the upstairs treadmills; and Felicia was en route to the dance studio, walking in the room with her Beyoncé confidence, ready to hit it to the music blaring through her headphones as she began her workout.

As she pumped and jumped, her breathing became heavy, and the sweating frenzy was in full effect. Tonight's workout was intense due to her thinking about her conversation with Derek that kept replaying over and over in her head. Trying her hardest to shake it from her mind, Felicia started her stretches off, bending and twisting certain parts of her body, when she noticed someone at the top window looking down on her. Felicia turned in the direction of the shadow form to get a better look as she wiped sweat from her face, but by the time she was focused, the shadow was gone. Looking around Felicia was thrown off a bit. She could of swore someone was there. Then she remembered. "You're fucking *high, Felicia,*" she said as she laughed at herself. Felicia let the paranoia sweat out as she went back into her routine with her dance. Thirty-five minutes later her Fitbit was going crazy. She had just reached a new level, and she was damn proud of herself and the work she had been putting in for the last six months.

Walking past the studio mirrors, she couldn't help but notice the changes in her body, a flatter toned stomach, a fatter and very firm ass, and legs to die for. She was very proud of the results. As she walked into the pool of the gym, she had a sick sense that someone was watching her. She stopped and turned toward the windows that hung over the pool, and to her surprise, no one was there. She turned in the direction of the sauna and headed to it. The closer she got, the stronger the feeling became. At this point she didn't know if it was the weed forcing her mind to play tricks on her or if she was just losing her mind. She decided to ignore the feeling in her gut and entered the sauna. Sitting on the bench she looked out at the pool and the whirlpool area. On any other night the pool area would be crowded with old-school men everywhere, but not tonight. The pool area was empty as hell.

Felicia thought about Derek and the last message he sent to her phone. *Why did I tell that psycho my fucking schedule? How could I be so stupid?* she thought out loud. She didn't know whether to be nervous or to just forget it. It was obvious that she couldn't do anything about it now because she already ran her mouth to this stalking motherfucker. Felicia's thoughts went from her messages to wondering how long Derek had been watching her before he went to prison. Unfortunately that was a question only Derek could answer, and in order to get the answer, she would have to get on Facebook and message him about it; but that wasn't a play she wanted to adventure into. She laid on the bench and covered her face with her towel and tried to clear her mind of the wicked thoughts she was having.

With her music blasted she was now comfortable with the fact that she was drowning out the sounds all around her including her thoughts. Felicia zoned so far out she didn't realize that Derek was right there in the gym with her and he was the one watching her while she danced in the studio room. He managed to lock both pool entrance and exit doors. No one could get in or leave out. Derek now had all the time he needed to do whatever he wanted with no distractions. He had his bag of goodies waiting for him in the sauna, and Felicia walked past everything without noticing. Derek sat on the bench across from Felicia watching her as she sang along with the music not realizing someone was in the room with her. Derek began to unpack his goody bag that he packed specifically for her. He removed a knife from his bag and placed it on the bench and then a bottle of chloroform to put her out and rope to tie her up.

Derek stood and placed his gun that was holstered in his pants on the bench next to the knife. He removed his shirt from his heated body as he walked over to the doorway and opened the door to the sauna, so some of the heat could escape out as he poured the chloroform on his shirt, and walked toward Felicia. She began to smell a weird scent, but before she could remove her towel to see who entered the sauna, Derek slammed his shirt over her face knocking her out.

Felicia woke up to music playing, but it wasn't in her ears anymore. It was now ringing from around the pool. He'd managed to black out all the windows on the second level, as if this was already something he had planned. She laid there trying to free her wrist, and that's when she heard a chuckle.

"*Who's there*?! Please tell me who you are!" Felicia shouted. The silence was driving her crazy as she began to cry. "Please tell me what you want."

A voice then said, "*You*! I've always wanted you, baby, but you always had to play hard to get. You know when you finally let me fuck you, Felicia, I couldn't believe it. I mean did you know how good your pussy felt on my dick, *girl*?! Then you just took it from me. That shit wasn't cool at all. You do know that, right?"

Before Felicia could say anything, he yanked her off the floor to her feet and placed tape over her mouth. She began sobbing more because Derek blindfolded her eyes, leaving her clueless to what was coming next. Derek then pulled out his knife and started rubbing it up and down her stomach. Felicia shivered as the cold steel pressed against her soft skin.

"You know," he said, "you haven't changed after all these years, baby. You're still beautiful as can be. Your body was tight the way it was, but it's even better with the weight loss you had."

Felicia moaned cries through the slits of the tape on her mouth as Derek seemed to get aroused by the sounds of her fear. He placed his body against hers and kissed her neck slowly while taking in her scent.

"Mmmm." He chuckled. "Baby girl, you smell fucking delicious." He began to laugh again. "How the hell do you remain fresh after a workout, baby? You smell like sweet sweat." He bit her ear. "I think I want to have some fun with you before I kill you," Derek stated.

Felicia cried harder as he laughed about her being helpless. With her hands and feet tied together in knots, there was nothing she could do to free herself from the hold Derek placed her in. She accepted her fate. Death was coming for her sooner than she thought.

"Please don't do this, Derek," she cried muffled words through the tape. "Please, Derek, you don't have to do this!"

"Baby girl, I can't understand when you muffle your words like that." He chuckled at her again.

He pulled her shirt over her head and dragged her back into the sauna.

"*Derek, please let me go*!"

"*Bitch*!" he growled. "Shut the fuck up. If you say another fucking word, you'll be losing a finger or a nipple!" Derek shouted at her.

Felicia got as quiet as she could with sniffling. She couldn't help but wonder how come her cousins hadn't tried to come to the sauna yet. Derek then pushed her down onto the benches in the sauna room.

"You know I really miss that cat, baby girl, and you're just giving it to that lame-ass nigga you call a husband. I can do way more for you than that bitch-made nigga. For example, if you were still mine, there's no way I would be letting you leave the house this fucking late and alone, baby girl. What kind of man lets his woman out of his sight with pussy that good? A fuck nigga—that's who, baby," Derek barked as he snatched the tape off her mouth.

"Derek, please I have money! I'll give you whatever you want. Just let me go. I have kids, Derek. Don't do this!" Felicia tried once more.

He then laughed and asked, "Will you suck my dick? Will you fuck me willingly like I were him? Maybe I'll let you keep your life."

Felicia began to cry again as Derek continued to laugh at the answer she was giving him in tears.

"Just as I thought. Now it's punishing time because I told you to shut the fuck up." *Wham!* Blood dripped from her mouth. "Now look at you. Shut the fuck up, so I don't have to hurt you before it's time." Derek then removed the shirt from her face completely but left the blindfold. "Lie down," he said with aggression.

Felicia laid back praying and hoping God wouldn't let her life end like this. She couldn't figure out what she had done so wrong to deserve this treatment. Derek started to kiss her sweaty stomach as he played with her nipples.

"See," he said. "You want this just as much as I do."

He pulled her shorts off along with her panties. Felicia shouted once more, "Derek, *don't do this*!" She cried more turning her head away from him. He put his face in her pussy and began to flick her clit with his tongue.

"*Mmmm*, you still taste good. I've waited for a long time to taste you, Felicia." He pushed his face deeper into her hot sweaty love spell.

Felicia tried to mask her moans, but it was really beginning to feel good to her as she wiggled away from him. Derek grabbed her hips and yanked her back to him. He enjoyed the sounds that escaped from her lips. It was turning him on more to hear her moaning out, and it was him who was causing her sweet melodies that graced his ears. His erection was at full attention because of her cries and sighs. When he stopped it seemed like everything around them had gone silent, and then she felt a cold sharp object touching her body again.

"I want to see you bleed more, baby girl." He slid the blade across her skin once more, this time pressing harder until she screamed out. "You taste like candy, baby. Your pussy is just as sweet as your blood is." He began to laugh.

"*You sick fuck*!" Felicia shouted. "*Let me go*! I swear you're going to regret this shit, you psycho *bitch*!"

"*Wow*, baby girl, tell me. What the fuck can you do?" He slammed the knife down next to her head. "Your hands and feet are tied, baby. The doors are locked. The windows are blacked out. Everybody in the gym can't hear you because the music is up and the pool is closed for cleaning. It's sad you didn't catch the sign on your way in. Now I got you all to myself." He grinned at her.

Felicia stopped crying as it made her feel weak and it seemed like the more tears she cried, the more he wanted her and tormented her. With a straight face Felicia said, "Hurry the fuck up and do what you got to do and get it over with."

With a laugh, Derek replied, "Oh, now you're rushing me, bitch." He repositioned her body against his, sticking his fingers inside her warm wet diligence pushing deep inside her and pulling out so slow and then forcing them back inside her world while tackling her sweet pearl. Derek watched the expressions on her face as she tried to fight the feeling of pleasure he was giving her body. Felicia hated that he was making her cum over and over again.

"Well," Derek said as he smirked at Felicia. "Baby girl, your pussy is so wet. I got to get in this shit." He slammed his thick lengthy cock inside her causing her to sound out from both worlds of tantalizing pleasure and pain combined. Derek stroked back and forth with his slow grind until she gave in and gave him what he wanted from her. Felicia started to rotate her hips matching his groove, clenching her honeydew around his hard erection causing him to sing with her harmonies.

Felicia was in hopes that if she could fuck back, Derek would come to his peak and it would all be over, but Derek failed to inform Felicia that he had taken a sustenance to keep him hard for the next hour, and that was way more than Felicia had bargained for.

She was used to the usual with her husband and the way he did things with her body. This was nothing she was used to at all. Derek was so different, fucking her hard while sucking on her nipple rings, then flipping her in different positions, slamming his cock back into her dripping wet pussy, pulling her hair, and slapping her ass. Felicia was cumming so hard from the roughness. This was definitely something out of the ordinary for her as he gripped her skinny neck with his big hands choking her and fucking her harder with each stroke.

Derek stared at her body as it synced with his. The moans triggered memories of the sex they had back in the day. He laid his head on and stroked as if he was making love grinding deeper and biting her neck. He was pleased when she climaxed.

"Damn, girl, you made a mess all over us," he said as he continued to stroke. Felicia's moans became enchanting to his ears as she sang sweet melodies of satisfaction.

Pulling out unexpectedly, he snatched Felicia off her back and onto her knees. Felicia heard a few moments of silence and tried to gather her thoughts on everything that was happening to her. Then suddenly she felt wet fingers rub up and down her asshole.

"Derek. No please, Derek. I've never done this, Derek. Please don't," she begged.

"I want that back shot, baby. Just relax, and it won't hurt much," he said as he chuckled at her.

"Please I'll do whatever else, just not this. It was feeling good in my pussy," she said trying to throw him off.

"What the fuck did I tell you about your *mouth*?! You go take this dick, bitch. I want you to feel every emotion you caused me. You're just getting yours in the physical form," he replied sticking a finger in her asshole.

Startled by the weird feeling, Felicia stiffened up locking her body. Her body ran hot and then cold instantly. Then she heard him say, "Relax, baby." Before she knew it his lengthy dick was forcing its way into her wet tight ass while he rubbed on her clit vigorously. She sobbed out loud trying to remember to relax, but the feeling was just too strong. It hurt and felt as if he was tearing her apart.

She'd never been introduced to anal sex before. She would shy of the thought when her husband would hit around to it, and now here it was—her first time on her knees on a sauna bench, partially dehydrated being fucked in the ass by her ex-lover she vowed never to fuck with for the rest of her days.

Derek worked his way in without causing Felicia too much pain; removing his hand from her wetness, he stroked very slow enduring the new adventure of her Krispy Kreme. He realized that she wasn't fighting him as much, so he picked up the pace going faster and harder. The feeling of pleasure turned into an uncomfortable plunge. Discomfort set in, and Felicia began to tense up. Felicia tried to sit up forcing him out of her asshole, but the more she tensed, the harder he went. Moans turned to cries of pain from the way he was fucking her. Unable to stomach the cries from a woman he was once madly in love with, he pulled his dick out. Felicia cried out. He grabbed his shirt and wiped his dick and noticed the bloodstains on the shirt making him feel low. He removed the blindfold from her eyes, so she could look him in his.

With her swollen red eyes, she stared back trying to focus, but all she had was a shadow image of his head.

"Untie me, Derek."

"No, I'm not done," he replied. "I only stopped because I wasn't ready for you to hurt that bad just yet." Although Felicia couldn't see his face, she could tell by the tone in his voice that he was lying to her. He still felt something for her, so why was he doing this to her?

"Derek, what are you going to do to me?"

Ignoring the question, he tossed the shirt to the floor and repositioned her onto her side.

Looking at her long toned legs and how far behind her head he could get them gave him the biggest stiff. He dug deep into that pussy. "I love this pussy, baby girl. I love you, and I want you to have my babies. That nigga needs to know I'm still in love with this little phat motherfucker, and it's all *mine. Uhhh*!" Driving his wood deeper and deeper, he busted his load inside her.

"Derek! *No*: *Nooo*! *Ahhhh*!" She came with him.

Derek laughed. "I thought you said you didn't want this? Bitch, you came like four times! Can that nigga make that pussy spit like I do?" he asked while rubbing her thighs. Felicia remained quiet, as she focused on his face again, asking herself what the fuck just happened. She couldn't believe she could come so many times at one time. She hated Derek, but he always knew how to trigger her sexy. She stared with confusion in her heart and jitters in her stomach as he continued to shove his gummy worm dick in and out of her sloppy wet pussy. She recapped moments of him being aggressive. Her body tingled from the thought. She liked it. Closing her eyes, she tried to shake the thought of the steel-cold object that rubbed across her stomach. Her body trembled more.

Jon noticed that two hours had gone by and they hadn't seen Felicia walk past the weight room nor had they seen her on the track, and that was the nightly routine. After grabbing Jay C's attention, they decided to head to the sauna while looking for their cousin who was MIA. When they arrived they saw a note on the door stating the pool area was closed for cleaning and heard the music blaring. Jay C walk to the dance studio to see if she would be in there. Jon was starting to get an annoying feeling in his gut that something wasn't right.

They walked at a faster pace to the other side of the gym, rushing through the door into an empty dance room.

"*Bruh*! Something doesn't feel right. Where the fuck is cuz at, bruh?" Jon said with clenched fist looking into the pool area.

"She got to be in that fucking sauna, but this motherfucking door is *locked*! What the ——!" Jay C yelled while snatching on the door handle.

Jon took a more focused look through the door and noticed a black hoodie next to the whirlpool. "*Aye, Felicia! Aye, bruh, that's cuz's hoodie.*"

Jay C continued to snatch the handle on the door as Jon got a weight from the rack and began to bust the window to get in.

Derek stood to pull his pants up over his semi-erect penis and smiled down on Felicia. She lay still on the bench. Her body was still sore and bloody. She was in shock about how her night turned out and how her body was completely drained. Still unable to see Felicia began to panic because she felt she should have had her sight by now. That's when she heard the barrel spin.

"That's the sound of a Revolver, baby. This will do some damage to that little body," he said.

Tired and refusing to beg for her life, Felicia closed her eyes and began to speak sense into the universe, praying that her cousins would find her soon because her life was about to end.

"You got any last words, baby?" Derek asked with hesitation in his heart.

A gunshot sounded, and Felicia thought her life was over. Then she heard another. The gunshots were all over the place. Jon and Jay C both made it in the sauna and got his ass before he could end hers. Jay C hit him in his head with a hand weight, and Jon followed up with punches.

The gun hit the floor when they were beating his ass. She strained hard to focus while she wiggled her hands free from the ties he had put her in. Then she noticed the gun right beside her on the floor. She came to a stand with noodle legs and a sore ass.

"*Derek*! *Derek*! *You sick fuck*!" she shouted as she pulled the trigger shooting him in the leg.

Derek fell to his knees smiling. "Bitch, I would never give you the *satisfaction* hearing me sound out. *Bitch*!" he growled.

"I don't give a fuck about you sounding out, fool. Just *fucking die, asshole*!" She pulled the trigger; Jay C knocked her hand in a different direction causing her to miss his head and shooting him in the shoulder.

"You stupid bitch, you should have killed me!" Derek said. Jon followed up with a kick to the face knocking him out, and Jay C phoned the police. Jon looked over at Felicia as she fell to her knees crying and still bleeding. Jay C helped her back to her feet so they could put her clothes back on her body while they waited for the police to arrive.

A week later news reporters were still trying to get in touch with Felicia about her gym rape that hit topline news, and to add she was suing the gym for negligence. Everywhere she turned there was something to remind her of the very thing she was trying her hardest to forget.

Felicia couldn't shake the fact that she was aroused by Derek's actions. Everything that he did to her was every fantasy she had for her and Ron. Felicia craved for Ron to be aggressive with her. She would daydream about his big hands around her throat as he pounded his girthy dick in and out of her pussy the way Derek did. Ron was not that kind of man. He couldn't let himself lose control with her. Their lives were casual sex. When Felicia would try new things, Ron would correct it. He didn't like new things; he liked his usual. Felicia knew he would never understand the new shit that graced her soul.

He would never understand taping her mouth and rubbing a blade around her titties and then sliding it softly across her nipples. The images stained Felicia's brain. She couldn't help but replay it in her mind like a broken record. Derek was in her head deep, the aggression, the way he growled at her, and the way he nibbled her earlobe as he pounded her pussy at close range. She critiqued his head, how he sucked on her clit bobbing his head up and down causing her to cum immediately. Felicia was definitely not in her right mind.

"Felicia," Ron called out to her snapping her back to reality.

"Yes, Ron," she answered.

"What are you thinking about, babe?"

"Nothing," Felicia responded to his question in a nonchalant tone. Ron could tell she was lying to him, but he didn't want to push her because of everything she was going through. As the married couple walked into the courtroom, Felicia locked eyes with Derek sending chills down her spine.

Her loins flamed for him. The stare was so hard and intense it made the jury uncomfortable. Ron snatched her close to him to gain control over his wife. Derek had awakened a demon inside her. Felicia broke eye contact when she bowed her head admitting to him that she was the submissive and he dominated her.

"How do you plead?" the judge asked.

"Not guilty, judge." Derek's cocky voice was burning bright in the courtroom.

Ron was pissed when they decided to take it to trial, yelling at the lawyers who worked for him. He demanded to know how the hell this was happening. Felicia had cuts to prove that he cut her, not to mention the gun that was on the scene belonged to him and her body still held his semen that they scraped out of her at the hospital! In disbelief Ron walked off throwing his hands in the air. He was lost, but he refused to sit around and let them blow through this case like it was nothing.

Six months went by, and Felicia seemed to be doing okay with the results of the trial. Derek had already been locked up for five months, but he'd received a sentence of three years. Felicia was just starting to turn back into her old self, but there was a part of her that she knew wasn't going to be normal ever again. Derek introduced her to everything she had only dreamed of. He'd blown her mind, and going back to vanilla sex would be impossible. How could she have regular sex with Ron when Derek was right there in the back of her mind driving her insides wild? That seemed to be the only conversations Felicia had with herself these days. Every time it crossed her mind, her pussy pulsated and throbbed. She'd have moments when she would get uncontrollably wet from thoughts of her and Derek in the sauna.

"Felicia. *Felicia*! Girl, don't you hear me calling you?" her mother, Sandy, said.

"Yes, Ma, what do you need?" Felicia responded as Sandy sat there looking at her daughter. Felicia began to laugh. "What, Ma? I did just ask you what you needed."

"I want to know what the hell got your mind so tough. I'm sitting right here next to your ass in this car and you can't hear me?" Sandy asked.

"Ma, I apologize. I've got a lot on my mind." Felicia sighed. "I'm dealing with these news reporters and everybody wanting to know how I've been doing since the situation that happened a few months back."

Sandy rubbed her fingers through Felicia's hair and asked her, "Well, how have you been, baby girl?" Sandy stated out of concern, "You don't talk much since it happened. You just sit around and stare out of whatever window you're sitting next to at the time. If something is seriously bothering you, baby girl, I really believe you should contact that counselor your doctor recommended."

Felicia was tired of everyone trying to help. What she really wanted was time to herself, but instead she was getting people telling her what was best for her and how she should just stay home from work until she was better mentally.

"You know, Ma, I'm fine and I wish you and everyone else would believe me. I understand it was a real shitty thing that happened to me, and I get it, but that doesn't mean that I have to roll over and play the damsel in freaking distress all the time. I have DJ's birthday coming up along with Jay C's prom, and Jon just started his new job working for the Miami Fliers training squad for college football, Mom. I don't have time to be selfish. I have to help my family get their shit together," Felicia replied to her mother.

Sandy drove in silence until they reached the airport. "Well, honey, I'm not trying to tell you how to live your life, nor am I trying to tell you how to run it, baby girl. I just want you to talk to someone if you need to. Don't let it ruin you. That's all I'm saying, okay?"

"Ma, if I need to talk to someone, I'm better off in your hands, not those quacks! I don't need to hear that I'm depressed all freaking day. I just have my own way of dealing with things, Ma, and you know that," Felicia responded to her mother.

"Yes, I know you do, baby girl. You are always my strongest child, always so independent, and doing things your way. You're a lot like your mother, baby girl," Sandy said with a smile. "Make sure to remind your father to pick me up Friday evening from the airport at 8:00 p.m. sharp and not a minute late either."

Felicia began to laugh at her mother. Sandy was just one of those women whom you didn't want to see angry nor be around.

Felicia gave her last goodbye hugs and kisses to her mother and then headed toward her sister's house for a slight gathering that she was putting together. Felicia decided to call her sister to see if she needed anything before she arrived.

"Hey, Heather, do you need anything for the gathering tonight?" Felicia asked.

"*Yes, boo,* I do. Could you please stop by the liquor store and grab three bottles for me? I need Hennessy, Crown Royal, and Courvoisier *please*!" Heather replied.

"Your ass always want the most expensive shit. *Damn*! Why you always got me breaking bread like I like you or something?" Felicia said as she chuckled.

Heather laughed through the speakers in the car. "Felicia, you know you love me, so stop playing," Heather responded to Felicia's joking comment.

"Yeah, yeah!" Felicia replied to her baby sister as she hung up the phone.

She headed into the liquor store to get the bottles for tonight's gathering when she caught a scent that jogged her memory of Derek. She began to look around the store trying to look for who was wearing the 1 million cologne. She was surprised when she was eye to eye with an old friend. "Yonni Johnson!" Felicia shouted as a big smile danced across her face.

"Hey, girl!" he said as he swooped her up in his arms. "How have you been?!"

"I've been better, but I guess I can settle for okay," Felicia responded. "So what are you doing back here in Dayton? I thought you moved to Miami, dude?"

"I did, shit." He laughed. "I came back because my little brother got a scholarship from Miami Fliers here in Dayton. We got to go through this training shit before they take him on fully," Johnson replied.

"Awe, *man*, that's great news. My little cousin just got the same thing come through for him. We have to be supportive for these young black men. They've come a long way from where we used to live!" Felicia replied.

"Shit, you can say that again, baby girl." He smiled with questions behind his gaze. "So, of course, I haven't seen you since that bullshit happened to you," Johnson said.

"Yeah, I know. I've been staying to myself because everybody has questions or something to say, and honestly, I've just been avoiding everything. I just want to go to work and home. Just know that I'm fine, Johnson. I'm dealing with shit one day at a time."

Yonni couldn't help but notice this glow that Felicia had about herself. "You know, Felicia, you're a gorgeous woman. I mean I thought you were going to be ugly, but you really filled out," Yonni said as he laughed trying to keep the conversation from going into the depression zone.

Felicia chuckled as they both filled the store with laughter. "Yeah, I bet, and I thought you were going to be like all the other broke brothers out here chasing after these big-booty Bettys in the streets," Felicia replied as Johnson laughed it off.

"It was really nice seeing you, Felicia. Keep your head up, baby girl," Johnson said as he walked out of the store.

Felicia went to the counter, so she could pay for the expensive items her sister had requested.

On her way to Heather's house, Felicia found herself thinking about the way Derek hit her and tasted her blood and then told her how sweet she tasted. What was really wrong with that sick fucker? *Why would he want to taste my blood?* she thought. As she arrived to Heather's house, she noticed Ron's vehicle was already outside with several others she didn't recognize.

Oh well, let's get this shit over with, Felicia thought out loud.

Walking into the house Felicia prepared herself for the evening and everyone with all their questions that they were about to unleash on her. As soon as she stepped foot in the house, Heather greeted her with a hug and walked her through the house to the kitchen where the rest of the ladies were. Heather introduced Sarah, Caria, Jasmine, Diane, and Shannon whom Felicia already knew.

"Hey, girl, how you been?" Shannon asked.

Felicia smiled and replied, "I've had better days." The girls laughed and continued the gossip.

Felicia and Heather were sitting side by side drinking, when their song, "Sexy and I Know It," came on. The party took a turn for the best. Everyone was enjoying life, and the best part for Felicia was no one was asking questions about her run-in with the psycho whom she had secretly fallen for all over again. The ladies lined up behind one another and went into the dance floor like it was their last night of freedom. Ron and the rest of the guys in the house couldn't believe what they were seeing; the girls were in the center of the living room grooving with each other putting on a show. Ron had never seen Felicia behave like this, especially not with another woman. He was in shock from the way she was acting when she began to grind on the other women as if they were the only ones in the room. He became uncomfortable from the way the girls were dancing, so he decided to step outside to clear his head. Ron couldn't figure out why Felicia was starting to act the way she was acting.

Although her rape situation happened six months ago, she'd been acting as if nothing happened to her at all. Felicia started going to strange clubs and hanging with people she wouldn't normally be with all hours of the night. Ron sat and thought about the amount of makeup she had started packing on. It was something she didn't normally do unless it was a special occasion, and the way she was starting to dress went against everything she stood for. Felicia's new wardrobe consisted of leathers and laces with push-up bras and tight-fitting pants or skirts and heels. She now wore different shades of black when she used to dress with color. Ron was not feeling the new Felicia nor the decisions she was making without even consulting him.

Felicia noticed that Ron was no longer watching her and the other females dance with each other, so she went to check on him and see what was going through his mind.

She stepped outside and found Ron sitting on the porch drinking his beer.

"Hey, baby, what's up?" she asked.

"Nothing, baby girl," Ron replied. His tone was dry, and she could tell something wasn't right with him; but she wasn't in the mood to be arguing about whatever was bothering him at her sister's gathering, so she kept it short with him.

"Well, since nothing is wrong, I guess we can head home and try that new bondage kit that we have. What do you say?" she inquired jokingly.

"You know, ever since that bullshit went on with you, you've been tolerating it really well. You want sex way more than usual these days, and then you're constantly stepping out the house with crazy-looking people; and you're gone half the fucking night, not to fucking mention when you leave you're dressed like a fucking *slut*! I must ask, Felicia: What the fuck is up with all this weird shit you are trying to do now? *I'm not fucking feeling it, Felicia*!" Ron replied with anger in his voice.

Stunned by the way he spoke to her, she just stood there for a few moments trying to gather her thoughts while processing everything he just said. Ron had never spoken to her like this.

"Ron, I don't know what the fuck you're going through, but ever since that bullshit happened, you've been treating me like I was the one who asked for it or something. You're always sitting around looking more depressed than I do when I'm the one whom that shit happened to! That shit plays in my mind all the fucking time. Did you ever think about that? Do you ever ask me how I'm feeling or what's on my mind? *Nah*, you don't because you're too busy seeing how I'm dressed like a slut and how I want to have sex with *my fucking husband*! If you're thinking somethine else, Ron, be a man and come the fuck out with it, hell, I'm already in a fucked up place in my life and the only thing that has been helping me through it is the weird fucking people whom you spoke of because the Lord knows my selfish fucking husband hasn't been there for me, *at fucking all*!" Felicia shouted.

The silence between the two became considerably uncomfortable. Ron threw the rest of his beer and walked off. Felicia turned and headed back to the house to grab her keys so she could go home when the girl she was dancing with met her at the doorway.

"Hey, beautiful," the stranger said.

Felicia turned and smiled at her and then greeted her, "Hello again."

"My name is Caria. Nice to meet you, Felicia."

"It was nice to meet you too," Felicia responded as she tried to get around Caria to get to the screen door.

"So we were dancing, and you just left me hanging, boo. What's up with that?" Caria said in a joking manner as she smiled at Felicia.

"My apologies, love, but I had to see what was wrong with my husband."

"Aww, is everything okay? Do you need a ride home or something?" Caria asked.

"No, I have a car, boo. I'm fine, but thanks for asking," Felicia replied once more.

"Well, do you mind if I walk you to your car? It's late, and you really shouldn't be alone out here. It's dangerous you know."

"The irony in that statement," Felicia implied as she laughed not touching the subject as to what she had just gone through. Although Felicia joked she wasn't aware that Caria had already been informed about the situation, but Caria wasn't going to mention anything if Felicia wouldn't.

The two ladies arrived at the car still in conversation about similar interests when Caria decided to ask Felicia out on a ladies' date night. From what just went on with Felicia and her husband, she needed some time away from reality, so they set a date to go out and get to know each other a little better.

A couple of weeks went by, and Felicia and Caria had been texting each other since the night of the party at Heather's house. The date arrived for the girls to go shopping and grab a bite to eat. Felicia was excited about the outing because Caria had become a good friend and an outlet for her. There was a knock at the door. Felicia called out for Ron to answer it and let Caria in. As soon as he opened the door, he locked eyes with a caramel smooth-faced green-eyed beauty. Caria smiled at Ron as she walked past him entering their home looking and smelling like a million bucks.

Ron was aware of Caria at the party that night. After all she was the main one grinding against his wife as he struggled to tear his eyes away from her. He never spoke of Caria, but he too thought of her often after that night. His heart raced with excitement as Caria walked through their house looking at the family photos. Ron already knew his marriage was on the rocks with Felicia, so he didn't want to add anymore strain on the relationship by getting caught looking at the only female friend whom Felicia decided to give a chance.

Caria decided she wanted to introduce Felicia to a whole new world tonight instead of shopping. Caria's heart was set on this club downtown in Indianapolis called The Leathery S&M. Caria begged and begged Felicia until she finally gave in and told her yes.

"*Omg, Felicia,* I swear you're going to love it!" Caria shouted with excitement. Felicia just smiled and nodded her head. Although Felicia told Caria yes, she really didn't feel like going to any clubs tonight. Felicia and Ron had a boring evening setup once she returned from shopping and eating. It involved sitting on the couch eating pizza and watching movies till they passed out for the night. 7:30 p.m. was approaching fast, and Felicia was still thinking of a way out of her and Ron's evening. Things were already in shambles, and they hadn't talked about the conversation at Heather's house a couple of weeks back.

The elephant in the room was in full effect, and no one was interested in addressing the problem at hand. Felicia was still upset at how Ron called her a slut in so many words, and Ron was becoming quite bored with Felicia and her new approach on life.

"Hey, babe, I think I'm going to take a rain check on our pizza night," Felicia said. Without mumbling a word Ron kept walking down the hallway as if he didn't hear Felicia speaking to him.

"*Did you hear me, Ron*?!" Felicia shouted.

"Yes, I heard your ass," he replied.

"So why didn't you answer me if you heard me, Ron?"

"I didn't think your statement needed an answer," he replied in a nastier tone.

Felicia stood there for a few moments thinking to herself if she should just go the fuck off on him now or wait until later. It was to the point where nothing she said or did for him made him happy. Ron seemed like he was always in a bitter mood, and Felicia couldn't understand why.

Felicia had made it through her situation alive without too much damage done to her physically, and Derek was now behind bars and wasn't getting out anytime soon. They were together and safe along with their children, all the bills were paid, and they both had good-paying jobs. So what the hell was Ron's problem? She turned and went back into her room while Caria waited in the living room.

"Hey, chick, are you about ready? You've been dressing yourself for an hour and a half now. *Damn*!" Caria yelled down the hall jokingly.

Felicia burst out laughing. "*Keep calm, boo*. I'm putting my warpaint on," Felicia replied as she finished up the last touches. She stepped out the room, and Caria was lost for words.

"*Bitch! You look amazing*!" Caria said in shock as she looked Felicia from head to toe.

Felicia smiled and replied, "Just the reaction I was looking for." The girls laughed together. "Ron, do you like it?" Felicia asked. He never looked her way. He just replied with a head nod. It was now, no doubt in Felicia's mind, that her and Ron were over. All the years of marriage and he was willing to throw it all away.

She couldn't believe he was treating her like this, but she refused to bring herself to an all-time low just because Ron was having trouble dealing with her being attacked at the gym months ago.

"Well, fuck you then. I'm out. And, no, you don't have to wait up for me because I'll be staying the night over at Caria's place," Felicia said in hopes of getting some type of reaction out of him, but Ron didn't respond or acknowledge that Felicia was even talking to him.

Felicia and Caria started out the door heading to the car, but Caria just had to ask, "Do you need to stay home tonight?" Caria said, "At least try to salvage what's left of your marriage, boo. It's not a problem for us to hang out another time."

Felicia laughed at Caria's suggestion. "I'm good, girl. He's been acting like that ever since that shit happened to me at the gym that night. But what I find so fucked up about it is he's treating me like I asked for that shit or something," Felicia replied. Caria sighed. "What, Caria?"

"Okay, boo, I'm about to be brutally honest with you. We've been cool for almost a month now, right?" Caria replied.

"Yeah, why are you asking me that though?"

"Well, it just doesn't seem like you've been down and out about it, boo. I mean granted I'm just getting to know you, but you just don't seem torn up about what has happened to you. Aren't rape victims supposed to act weird toward men and sex?" Caria asked with a more concerned tone in her voice.

"I don't know," Felicia responded to all the questions she was being bombarded with. "I find myself thinking about certain things that were done to me, Caria, but what's strange is I don't hate Derek. I actually think about him often. I think about the way my body responded to him. I even get turned on thinking about how he did me. I'm fucked up, aren't I?" She dropped her head and began to cry about it.

"*Hold up, bitch*! I didn't mean for you to get all emotional on me and shit. You better stop being a little pussy!" Caria stated in a joking manner.

Felicia laughed as she wiped the stream of tears that were flowing. She had never been close to any outside females, and now here she was getting close to Caria a lot faster than she thought.

"I know you have been through it, boo, and I get you not wanting to talk about it, but have you ever thought to yourself maybe Derek gave your body what it'd been missing and maybe this is the real you and he just opened Pandora's box?" Caria asked as she waited patiently for a response.

Felicia couldn't answer because she had not a clue on what she wanted or liked. All she knew was that her body had an appetite and she had no clue on how to satisfy the cravings. She sparked the blunt and blew smoke as they continued their way to the spot Caria wanted so desperately to introduce her too.

Stepping into the club all Felicia saw was fog and smoke and blinking lights. The club was packed with half-naked bodies and masked faces. It was most definitely something different for Felicia.

Caria headed straight to the bar for drinks, while Felicia, still stunned, took the place in. The scenery was something amazing. She had never seen a place like this; people were swinging from the ceiling and all over each other on the dance floor. As she stood in the middle of the dance floor smiling at the leather-masked people, she noticed someone standing in the midst staring at her. Confused by what this person was, she turned and walked in Caria's direction. Then her jam came on and stopped her: Maroon 5's "Animals." This was Felicia's favorite song, and she always went hard when it played at the gym. How would she control herself? High off the bud she and Caria had smoked in the car, Felicia's hips seemed like they had developed a mind of their own. Her body swayed with the beat as the masked stranger appeared closer than the last time. She closed her eyes for a few seconds and opened them back, and the stranger was gone. Felicia gazed through the crowd of people, but it was too late. He'd seemed to have disappeared. She turned to walk off the floor, and there he was, standing right in front of her.

The masked stranger rubbed the leathery suit against Felicia's soft, smooth skin, their bodies in sync as they swayed with the music. Without hesitation Felicia placed her hands on his chest. The heat from his body inside the suit warmed her almost instantly as she looked back at him catching a gaze in his eyes. This was something different, and she wanted to welcome the masked stranger with every adventurous inch he could supply her with.

Caria approached the dance floor with their drinks, and just like that he was gone again.

"Who was your friend?" Caria yelled.

"I have no idea, but that was some intense shit. His body was amazing in that suit!" Felicia replied with a huge smile.

They looked around for him in the crowd, but there was no sign of the masked stranger. Felicia tried to remain calm and cool throughout the night, but the image of the stranger kept creeping back into her mind causing her night to be interrupted. She wanted to know whom this person was and why he chose to imprint himself on her.

She scanned the dance floor once more in hopes that he would be there watching her, but he was gone, and so was the thrill about this place. They left the dance floor and had a seat at the bar.

"Maybe it was just my imagination playing tricks on me, Caria. I mean that was some good ass bud you had me choking on," Felicia said as she chuckled.

"Girl, that bud was good but not that damn good. That sexy motherfucker was there, and that body was on point; so if you imagined it, we imagined the same shit," Caria replied as they both laughed.

"Hey, boo, I'm about to hit the ladies' room real quick. I'll be right back," Felicia said.

"Do you need me to come with you?" Caria responded.

"No, babe, I'm good, but you can be on the lookout for our masked man," Felicia joked as she walked away.

Heading into the ladies' room, Felicia noticed that her mascara was starting to run from the heat in the club. After getting her makeup together, Felicia headed out the restroom to join Caria again, when she bumped into someone who was outside of the ladies' restroom.

"Hello," he said.

"Hello yourself," Felicia replied as she smiled at the handsome face that was greeting her.

"You don't recognize me, do you?"

Felicia stood there and then replied, "I'm sorry. Should I?"

"It's me, the guy whom you were dancing with."

Here he was right in her face with his mask off. She couldn't believe how handsome he was. She had a chance to take in the whole package. She swallowed hard as he stared at her with fire in his eyes. He sent chills to her soul from the connection they had with just their eyes. He was tall with a slender build. His teeth so perfect and white as he shined that beautiful smile at her, the waves in his hair, the smooth caramel skin tone—this was God's creation, and it was a very magnificent one.

"Oh my, my friend is waiting for me. I have to go," she said as she tried to escape from his tantalizing glare.

"Hey, before you run off and do the whole Cinderella thing, answer me this: Do you really have to go, or are you just running from me?"

She laughed. "Why would I be running from you, sir?" Her heart thumped in her throat from the nervousness he was causing. "Look. You're handsome, but I can't do this. I'm married, so I can't do this," she replied repeating herself.

"Do what?" he replied and flashed another smile.

"*Do this*! Whatever this is going to turn into, I can't do it."

"I just wanted to introduce myself. That is all." He smiled again. "My name is Derrell."

The name rolled off his tongue, and she couldn't help but notice how clean-cut his goatee was. His eyes were sexy enough to make you melt if you stared too deep into them. She tried again to pull herself out of his trance, but she didn't get too far. His face was now engraved in her brain. She stopped in her tracks. *I'll see this man one last time, and then I'll be done*, she thought to herself. She turned back in his direction to face him. She locked eyes with her masked stranger. Derrell had put his mask back on, and she was looking at a fully dressed S&M character.

She knew being attracted to him was wrong, but him being in that suit was just all-out fucked up. Her insides quivered with excitement. Something told her to keep walking, but she was done running from the things that excited her most. She wanted to know him and everything he could introduce her to. As she invaded his space, she looked deep into his eyes. The club seemed as if it went silent because all she could hear was the racing of her heart, and then she touched his suit to feel the smoothness of it as he caressed her back. Every touch felt like it was sending shock treatment to her. She gazed back into his eyes and wondered if he could feel what she was feeling. She felt connected to this man, but then she let all the bad in with the good. How many times would he do this a night? And how many women he'd made feel like this? And what if he liked men too? The connection was over, and she let go and turned to walk away.

She felt a tug on her hair, and before she knew it she was in his arms, and his lips were on her neck. Then he whispered in her ear, "I don't give two fucks about your husband, baby. The fact that you're here and he's not lets me know that you're neglected, in *both* places." He cuffed her pussy tight in his hands. She tried not to look at him, but he was in full control with a tight hold on her hair and pussy. She couldn't turn away and he knew she didn't want too. The shit he was saying rang like a church bell on first Sunday. Ron hadn't had sex with her in over six-and-a-half months. Her body was long overdue for an orgasm.

"Derrell, please let me go," she said.

"Why, baby? You don't like this?" He tugged harder on her hair causing her to moan out.

"Umm, I can't, Derrell. This is very tempting, but like I said, I'm umm…I'm umm…"

"I think the word you're looking for is married," Derrell replied as he chuckled in her ear. "Do you really want me to stop, baby? I will if you really say it like you mean it." He caressed her pussy with his fingers.

Felicia's breathing became heavy as her heart thumped harder and harder in her chest. Her thoughts were all over the place.

"Derrell, this is wrong! I can't. Please just let me go," Felicia moaned at him.

"Nah, not convincing enough, baby girl. All I heard was keep going, and the fact you're no longer putting up a fight furthers the situation. How experienced are you? Are you experienced enough to satisfy me, baby?" Derrell questioned as he stroked with his magical fingers. "What's your name?" he whispered softly as he continued to massage.

"It's umm…It's umm…*Felicia*!" she said with a gasp. "Oh god, could you let go now?"

"Hey, Felicia, it's nice to meet you, baby doll," he said rubbing his mask across her face. "Your pussy feels like it's soaked." He went into her pants for further detailing. His fingers glided across her pussycat like he had been there before playing with her clit as they swayed to the only music she was making and then penetrated into her world. "That pussy is tight. I know it's good, and it's not even on my dick yet."

Felicia's body and mind were now at attention. He was more than what she could handle. The stroke of his fingers entering her pussy and massaging her clit had her on edge and ready to cum. "Derrell, stop. You have to stop."

"Why stop when it's feeling so good to you? The way your body is responding to me, I would say you haven't been touched in a long time, baby doll. I can make you cum if that's what you want."

"No, it's not what I want. I want you to let go." Felicia sighed.

"Baby doll, if you really wanted to go, you could have left at any time. I'm not a rapist," Derrell responded. "I'm just here to give the ladies what they want, what they crave. All of you married chicks who come here just want to be fucked. I read you like an open book when you entered my club, baby. You're craving for my dick to bless your insides right now. You act like you don't want it, and you say stop in a way that screams to me that you want more." He pushed his fingers deep into her juicy piece of fruit. "I don't understand." He bit her neck. "Why come to a place like this and try to play that innocent role acting like I make you nervous or something when in all actuality you're the biggest freak in this place. With my help you could become a very intimidating dominant, baby doll. I mean look at you. You're standing here with your body against mine wanting to be fucked lifeless." Felicia came from the tension that built up. Then she stood in silence for a minute, stunned that this stranger was speaking the truth and offending her at the same time.

"Like I said in my head, I'm tired of running from what excites me most. Tonight it changes. Yes I need to be fucked, but do I want to be fucked by you. NO! I have a dick at home," Felicia responded sounding as confident as she could.

Derrell began to laugh at her. "Baby, everybody who comes in here is looking for some type of fantasy. I could tell you yours if you'd like to hear it," he said while still thrusting his fingers in and out of her pussycat with more aggression.

"What's my fantasy, Derrell?" Felicia moaned while looking deep into his piercing hazel eyes. "What the hell do you think you know about me? *Oh god! stop*!" Felicia came harder the second time around and her body went limp in his grips.

He kissed her neck and laughed. "Baby doll, that's not fair at all. You came twice. I said you could come one time. I never told you to cum again, but since it's your first time, I'll let you slide. Go clean yourself up. I'm sure your friend is looking for you by now." He pulled his fingers out of her pussy and walked off leaving her there with her thoughts about her fucked up side that just revealed itself in a flashing fogged hallway near bathroom stalls.

Meanwhile, Caria was at the bar in deep conversation with the bartender about job openings that had come available in the club and how much each position made. Felicia had to clear her head before she could return back to the bar. In the restroom she caught a glimpse of herself in the mirror. Not ashamed of anything that just happened, she smiled. Who the fuck was this man who just made her cum from practically doing nothing? He would now invade her personal brain space all night thinking about the adventures he could bring her if they were to ever meet again. She wondered how he could read her so easily in so little time. He was a very attractive devil, and she wanted more.

After a long night with Caria, it was time for Felicia to return back to work for this long dreadful week that was ahead of her. While scrolling through social sites, Felicia couldn't help but think about Derrell. She was caught up in the way he bit her neck and maintained his magical finger work on her pussycat. *Whom am I turning into? Why would I let some stranger put his hands on me like that? What's worse why was I enjoying it so much. I mean I really enjoyed myself in his arms, the way he pulled my hair as I rubbed on his muscular body*, Felicia thought to herself.

The questions burned on Felicia's mind all day. Whom was she turning into, and why was this type of sexiness getting into her?

Ring! Ring! Her phone jolted her back to reality for just a few minutes.

"Hello," she answered not even looking at the caller ID.

"So you thought that shit was cute not coming home last night?" Ron responded in a bitter tone.

"Ron, I don't have time for this. I'm working," Felicia scowled at him.

"Felicia, I don't want to do this anymore. I want my wife back. What's going on with you?" Ron replied sounding more concerned this time.

"Didn't I just tell your ass I'm at work and I don't have time for this right now? When I wanted to talk to your ass at my sister's house, you could care less about what the fuck I had to say. But as soon as I stayed away from home, that's when you want to act all concerned. Miss me with this *bullshit, Ron*!" Felicia snapped and ended the call.

Ron dropped the phone and sat on the edge of the bed holding his face as he cried. He was losing his wife, and he couldn't understand why he was being made out to be the bad guy.

Listening to the dial tone, Ron pulled himself together. Picking up the phone he decided to call Sandy to see if she had spoken to Felicia and if she planned to leave him because she damn sure wasn't sharing anything with him. Ron and Felicia had been best friends for over fifteen years. They shared everything with each other whether it was good or bad.

Ron wiped his face as he thought about their vows. They promised to always talk about what they felt, and for some reason Felicia wasn't holding up on her end of the bargain. She was hiding something from him, and Ron was determined to find out what the hell it was that had his wife acting out of the ordinary.

Sandy answered with a soft tone, "Hello, Ron. To what do I owe the pleasure?"

Ron laughed and replied, "Hello, Mom, how are you?"

"I'm fine, Ron. And yourself?"

"I've been better, Mom."

"Uh-oh, that's not good. Well, let's get it off our chest, Ron. What's the problem?" Sandy asked concerned.

"Yes, ma'am. I was wondering if you could tell me what's going on with Felicia. She's shutting me out, and I don't understand why, Mom. I've been a good husband. I go to work and help pay the bills. I help put food on the table, and I take care of her and the kids, Mom. I mean anything she needs or wants, I bust my ass to give it to her, and right now I really don't know what to do. I feel like I'm losing her." He broke down for a second time on the phone with Sandy this time.

Sandy was at a loss for words. She had no clue why Felicia was acting the way she was. Sandy was hoping Ron could tell her something, but they were in the same boat. Sandy explained to Ron that Felicia hadn't been talking to her like she normally did and she knew something was wrong. She just didn't realize things had gotten so bad between the two of them. Sandy offered her advice to Ron on what he should do.

"Give Felicia her space until she is ready to talk to you about what's bothering her. If you continue to push, she's going to pull away from you, Ron." Sandy said her goodbyes, and they hung up the phone.

Ron was listening, but this was nothing he was used to at all. He was used to talking their problems out whenever one would occur. They'd resolve it and move on. They had never gone to bed with unresolved issues, let alone going out and staying away from home all night. There was definitely something wrong, and Ron was willing to get to the bottom of it.

As the day went on, Felicia was thinking about the way she treated Ron. *Why was I being such a bitch to him? I've known this man half my fucking life. When I wanted to talk about everything and lay it all on the table, he was too busy calling me a slut. So I can imagine what the fuck he'll think if I express to him the things that interest me these days. I'm scared of being judged by the person I love the most, but even more terrified to let him see whom I'm turning into. He'll pack his bags and leave me and the kids so quick. He can't even handle my clothes. How on earth will he be able to handle cuffs, ropes, leather whips, and chains?* Sick with the thoughts that made her loins burn, Felicia shook the thoughts away along with telling Ron her darkest fantasies.

Caria sat at her kitchen table going through her tarot cards, shuffling the deck and smiling as she flashed back to the time she spent last night with Felicia. It had been awhile since she had a female friend whom she actually liked and wanted to be around. She flipped over the first card with Felicia still in mind. Caria decided she would do a reading on Felicia. What was she looking for in her future was revealed in the first card, the Fool, meaning new beginnings as well as the purity and open-hearted energy of a child. Caria found this card to be positive as she smiled and pulled the next card, the Hermit, an extremely spiritual card often having to do with being introspective, thinking things over, or seeking a greater understanding.

Pulling the next card Caria saw the Lovers. This card indicated a moral or ethical crossroad, a decision point where you must choose between the high road and the low road. Frowning her face Caria felt this card could represent your personal beliefs because to make a decision you must know where you would stand. She believed that following your own path could mean going against those who were urging you in a direction that was wrong for you. Caria's thoughts quickly switched to Ron's behavior before they left the house. *Is he the wrong path in Felicia's new world?* she wondered.

The last card completing the four-card draw sent chills down Caria's body: *Death.* Death often represented an important ending that would initiate great change. It signaled the end of an era, a moment when the door was closing. At such times, there could be sadness and reluctance but also relief and a sense of completion.

Dying had a way of making you concentrate on what's important, and revealing this card made Caria go into panic mode. She'd never pulled Death on anyone before whether they were present or not. Caria was already concerned about Felicia, but now it would turn to worrying about her new friend on a constant basis. *Ring*! *Ring*! The phone startled Caria out of her paranoia.

"Hello," Caria answered.

"What's up, love? What do you got going on tonight?" the voice asked.

"Who is this?" Caria replied.

"It's me, goofy-ass girl. Sage! Guess you wouldn't know me anymore since you got a new friend whom you're hanging with," Sage replied with a jealous tone.

Caria began to laugh. "*Sage*! You will get a chance to meet Felicia, girl, and please don't be tripping because Felicia isn't even like that."

"Girl, bye. Nobody is tripping, and what do you mean she isn't like that? Girl, *please*! Everybody is like this. They just don't want to be real with themselves!" Sage replied sounding less jealous.

Caria sat on the phone laughing at Sage because she knew there was a part of her that wanted to go all the way with Felicia, but she didn't know how she would react if she made a pass. Caria wasn't ready to spoil their friendship over their beliefs of what's right and what's wrong. Caria and Sage continued to plan their next outing, but this would be an outing that Felicia wouldn't be able to join. Caria new that Sage wasn't ready for the competition, and Caria wasn't ready to put Felicia in an uncomfortable situation.

"Sage, what are you planning to wear?" Caria asked.

"Umm, I was thinking all black," Sage replied.

"*Yes*, like your heart," Caria replied jokingly as they both chuckled. "Naw, I asked because I got this black fitted *Ed Hardy* minidress, and I didn't want to be the only one dressed like a whole lot of fun. Feel me?" Caria responded.

"Girl, I got an *Ed Hardy*, but it's colorful. Where the hell did you find a black *Ed Hardy* dress?" Sage asked out of concern.

"Girl, I didn't. When I came home last night, there was a package waiting for me, so I opened the shit. Inside was a dress, and get this, Sage. There was no address on whom it came from or anything."

"You better make sure there are no damn bugs on it or someone is not trying to set you up! You put that damn dress on, and all your skin falls the hell off!" Sage replied.

Caria laughed hysterically. "What the fuck is wrong with you, Sage?! My skin falls off? Really?" Caria laughed again. "I've tried the dress on too many times already, boo, and my skin is fine."

"You can't be too careless these days," Sage replied as she laughed along with Caria.

"Well, it fits, boo, and I look good in it too. You'll see it once you get here, but before we get into that, do you mind if I unload some stuff in your lap?" Caria asked.

"Sure, boo, go ahead."

"Well, I was doing the cards, and I decided to do Felicia."

"Wait. What?" Sage replied.

"I know. I know."

"You know you're not supposed to pull the cards on people unless they say you can, Caria. Why would you do that?" Sage replied with an angrier tone.

"I just wanted to see what the cards would say, Sage." Caria's tone went dry.

"What the hell did you pull, Caria?"

"The first card was the Fool."

"Which means what, Caria?" Sage asked as she interrupted Caria before she could name the second card.

"It means she could be taking her first steps toward fulfillment and completion; do you mind if I move along, or do I need to tell a full story on this one as well?" Caria replied.

"Don't be mad at me! If you came to the sessions on a regular basis, I wouldn't have to question you to make sure you're properly educated on what the hell you're doing!" Sage responded sounding even more irritated with Caria.

"The second card was the Hermit. I find this one to be like the Fool, but it's a necessity to be alone so she could figure out where or what path to take. Card 3 was the Lovers card."

"Aww, you're saying it like it is a problem, Caria. Damn!"

"Well, you didn't let me finish, Sage. The last card I pulled was Death," Caria replied.

"Hold up. So you're telling me that not only did you pull cards on a bitch you don't really know but you pulled a four card without even getting her consent on it. What made you pick that number, Caria?" Sage asked, lost for words.

Caria responded, "I don't know, Sage. It just kind of happened. I was cool until Death hit my table. I know the readings, but like I said Death shook me."

Sage could hear Caria's sincerity. "Oh, relax, motherfucker. It's not like death is the end of her. Death has several meanings." Sage sighed. "Look, Caria. In readings Death often represents an important ending that will initiate great change. It signals the end of an era, a moment when one door is about to shut. You get what I'm saying, love? There may be sadness and reluctance but also relief and a sense of completion. It's a truism in tarot work, Caria. That card 13 rarely has anything to do with physical death. A responsible card reader never interprets card 13 in this way because its view is too limiting. Death doesn't just happen once to our bodies. It happens continually, at many levels and not just in the physical. We die each moment in the present, so the future can unfold. You would know this if you came to the sessions though," Sage griped.

"I know, Sage. I was bored, and hell you pull cards on people all the time without their approval, so what the fuck is wrong with me doing it?" Caria replied in a bitter tone.

"Let's see why an unexperienced tarot reader shouldn't pull cards on people. Umm, I got it—*because they don't know what the fuck they're doing*!" Sage replied filling the phone with laughter. "Everything will be alright. After all the card could have been for you."

"Why the fuck would you say something like that, Sage?!" Caria yelled.

"Because you need to learn everything isn't meant for you to know. I mean what else did you think was going to happen? You read her cards and everything would be okay? You've only known this chick for a few weeks, and you are bopping like you've known each other for years, face-ass bitch!"

"Sage, she is just a friend." Caria laughed. "There is no need to get in your feels, damn girl. I like her, but I like you more; however, you need not to forget that you are my teacher. We are not exclusive, and I also pay for my sessions, so the professional thing to do in a situation like this is cut out any emotion-causing ties and continue our sessions until I reach a full understanding of everything," Caria stated.

Sage sat in silence for a few moments. "I can teach you whatever you're willing to learn, and I know you love me. I just also know your love isn't the same as my love for you, Caria. You re such a free spirit, and I know it's hard to tame a free spirit; and honestly, boo, I wouldn't want you tamed because then your flame would burn out, Caria. We all know that's what attracted me to you, that *flare*! I know how to fall back though."

The phone went silent for few seconds before Caria finally replied, "Did you just give me a compliment in the same sentence you called me a hoe?"

They both laughed hysterically. "I like my phrase better, Caria. You're a free spirit, babe, and that's okay!" The laughter continued. The conversation between the two went on for another half an hour, until Caria realized it was past 4:00 p.m. and she's already behind schedule.

"Sage, I have to go. My meeting with the staff at the club is in thirty minutes! See you at the club tonight, babe," she said as she slammed the phone on the hook and rushed to the shower. After only a few seconds of water hitting her smooth skin, she was back out the shower drying off. Caria was moving as fast as she could when the house phone rang again. "*Don't answer that, Caria*! Get your fat ass in these jeans!" she shouted as she tugged at the tight jeans trying to get them up her damp thighs. She wiggled and wiggled until the jeans were over her plump ass.

She threw her half-cut sweater over her head and grabbed her shoes and headed out the door.

She hopped in her car and sped through the streets of Indianapolis arriving just in time at her destination, The Leathery S&M.

"Hello, Mr. Werth, I'm sorry I'm late. I got into a family situation, and time got away from me," Caria responded immediately.

He stood there looking at Caria because he had no clue as to whom she was and why she would be late to a meeting with him. Stunned by her beauty he decided to have this meeting to see where it would go and what Caria was all about.

"So how long have you lived in Indianapolis?" Werth asked.

"I've lived in the area for about five years, sir," she replied. He began to chuckle. "Is something wrong, sir?"

"Yes, you keep calling me sir like I'm my father or something," Werth stated.

A slight cut of the eye, Caria responded with a firm tone, "My apologies. I just assumed that you would be my boss, and I wanted to show the proper respect. I mean not that I'm not proper. I just—"

"You need to calm down," Werth said. "Take a deep breath and blow it out, love."

Caria stood there looking for a few seconds and then took his advice into consideration. She felt jittery, and now she was starting to stutter not sure if he was giving her attitude or not, so she filled her lungs with air and exhaled. She felt the tension escaping from her body.

Werth's eyes were locked. She stood 5′6″ with a slim waist. He couldn't help but smile when he scanned lower to her thighs. "You're a very beautiful woman. I love how smooth your skin looks. Is that your real hair?" Werth asked.

"I'm sorry. What?"

"Your hair, is it real?" Werth asked again.

"Umm, yes, it is. I didn't have time to do it." She rubbed her fingers through her natural curls.

"You know what. The job is yours under one condition," Werth said.

"And what's that?"

"Please don't be so quick to jump to defense mode, gorgeous lady. It throws you off your A game. Feel me?" Werth replied and smiled.

Caria went from caramel to cherry red. He was flirting, while she was enjoying that smile that he flashed her. She had no idea that she was meeting the masked man that she and Felicia saw a few nights back, but for Derrell, it was just now syncing. He knew she looked familiar, and at first he thought maybe she just had a familiar face, but that wasn't the case. He had watched her and her friend that whole night.

"So when could you start? Well, hold on. What position are you applying for?" Derrell asked.

"Well, the gentleman behind the bar told me I would be used for bartending."

"You sure? I could definitely use someone with your physique in one of my cages, doll." Derrell smirked.

Caria smiled. "Thank you, but, no, I can't dance and that would be a big mess." She continued to laugh. "I do have my bartending license if you like to see them," she responded, ruffling through her purse to get her ID.

"What a loss then. That could have been something amazing to look up and see," Derrell stated as he looked at her license.

"As soon as you need me, Mr. Werth, I'm available."

His eyebrow lifted.

"I mean for the job, sir, to bartend."

"I got it, love." He smiled more still examining her license.

Caria chuckled; she couldn't believe that this was the interview. It was more like flirting and cheesy sparks flying between the two, but she knew she couldn't question anything because rent was due and the tarot readings weren't bringing the dough in like it once was.

"So you'll start tonight behind the bar and hopefully broaden your levels in the future. The cage starts off at fifty dollars an hour. Bartending is only thirty-five dollars; however, you have a splendid body. Hopefully you can dress the part. I can see you dominating the tips."

"Thank you. I'll be here tonight at ..."

"Nine forty-five sharp. I like to go over something with the staff before I unleash them upon the night," Derrell said and chuckled. Caria laughed at the weird moment she thought they were having, but she was bursting with excitement for landing this job. Taken by Caria's smile Derrell paused and just stared. "Your teeth are so white. My god, girl, you have a killer smile. I think I should just keep you as a secretary. What do you think? Could I have you all to myself, Caria?"

Caria stood in silence unsure of what to say. He had already crossed the line so many times she felt as if she was being tested or something. She smiled more a sensual smile and lifted her brow just like his and took control of the situation.

"I'm standing on my word, Mr. Werth. I'd like to bartend in my skimpy little whatnots, and if in the future I need a promotion, I promise I'll be the girl to bring you to your knees, papi." She slid her fingers across his zipper.

"Well, that's good to know. Bring that spirit and highlight your sexy, baby!" Derrell replied kind of shaken over what just took place. That was the first time a female had ever challenged him back.

They continued the interview with Derrell walking her throughout the club showing her the areas that she would have access to and the places that were off-limits to her until her ninety-day probation period was up. After showing Caria everything there was to show, Derrell ended the interview and told her he would see her later in the evening for training. Derrell walked off leaving Caria standing there with her thoughts of him.

"Damn! Was that the interview?" she asked herself. "A bunch of flirting and hygiene questions? Shit! If every job did interviews like that, I'd be a fucking millionaire," Caria ranted to herself as she turned and headed back to her car. Getting into the vehicle her phone began to ring. Looking at the screen she locked her seat belt.

"Hey, boo, how are you doing?!" Caria shouted through the phone lines filled with excitement.

"I'm not good, Caria. My fucking car won't start, and I'm already late as fuck for work, and on top of that this nigga over here is tripping. I just really need you right now, Caria," Felicia responded. The transmission had finally gone out in the Grand Prix dropping her and Ron down to one vehicle. With Ron and Felicia working on opposite sides of town, it put more strain on top of them.

They both could only be late so many times before one would be fired bringing the household down to one steady income. That was the last thing they needed in their life, and Felicia was trying her best to handle it by not snapping at her husband who she could see was really trying for his family. Caria could hear the shakiness in her voice that she was trying to keep it together, so she didn't want to spring up her good news when her friend was having a bum-ass day.

Caria suggested that she should take the day off. It didn't seem like a good idea for her to head to work with the type of mood she was in. Caria drove from the club straight to Felicia's house while trying to keep her calm and away from Ron. Caria knew the situation, and she liked Ron and Felicia together. They were real lovers in her eyes who just had some kinks that needed to be ironed out. Pulling out of the driveway, Ron slowed down because a vehicle was slowly approaching his house. Ron came to a complete stop as the vehicle came closer. Caria smiled as he watched her like a hawk parking her car beside his and then getting out. Ron was waiting for her to turn his way, but Caria kept her face forward walking toward the house. Ron swallowed hard as she walked up to the front of his door to greet Felicia. He didn't understand this feeling she was causing him to have toward her. He stared a few minutes longer and then proceeded out the driveway.

It had been a busy day already for Caria, and now she would spend the next hour playing counselor.

"Everything is going to be alright, Felicia. You just really need to calm down, boo. Take a deep breath and blow it out and please let me tell you about my day. Then we can finish the rest of the afternoon discussing your issues. That way I can be on time for work tonight at eight," Caria said as she smirked at Felicia.

"Awww, *bitch*! *You got the job*! Why didn't you text me and tell me you had the job? I wouldn't have been telling you about all my bullshit! *Shit*! That's great news, Caria. I'm so happy for you, boo."

Felicia hopped off the bed and tackled Caria with a huge hug knocking Caria off-balance dropping them straight to the floor.

"I'm glad you're happy for me, babe, but I believe you're crushing my vagina with your knee," Caria responded.

"Oh, I'm sorry." Felicia laughed.

"No, you're fine. I just might want to use little nanny again someday," she mouthed the words to Felicia while laughing.

"So what was the interview like?"

"It was cool I guess. It wasn't really an interview, boo. It was just a bunch of flirting and hygiene questions and shit like that," Caria replied.

"What?"

"Yes, girl, he wanted to know if I had ever had braces and complimented me on how straight and white my teeth were. Then he was telling me I smelled good and how clean and inviting he liked his employees to look to the public."

Felicia couldn't control the laughing any longer. She had to let it out. "Girl, you got a freak for a boss."

"I know, but he's so ding-dang delicious. He's handsome with a clean-cut hairline, not to mention he wears a suit like it's nobody's business," Caria replied.

"*Hmmm*, sounds like fun. Are you guys hiring?" Felicia said jokingly.

"Girl, stop talking shit. You know damn well you aren't about to leave that funky-ass airport," Caria replied laughing at Felicia.

"I just might! You think I'm playing? How the hell do I get an application then, heffa?! I'll fill it out," Felicia replied sounding convinced.

"I tell you what. Since you're talking shit, you can come to the club with me tonight, and I can see if Werth would be willing to hire you right on the spot. And, yes, that means you need to look the part," Caria replied.

"Look the part?" Felicia asked.

"Yes, look the part, which means no cute jeans or cute boots with a cute top," Caria replied.

"Damn, bitch! Why do you keep saying cute like it's a bad thing or something?" Felicia responded, irritated with the word cute.

Caria could see that she had gotten under Felicia's skin, and that's exactly what she was aiming for. It was something about Felicia. Once she got mad you could pretty much get her to agree with anything you'd say just for her to be hip. Caria pegged it and used her weakness against her.

"Cute is bad at the S&M. I need sexy, confidence, and fierce," Caria said.

"I have those things," Felicia said almost like she was asking a question.

Caria smiled. "Boo, you're innocent, and that's cool because you have lots of potential."

"I want to be those things, Caria. I'm just different."

"I see it in you. You just got to learn to let it shine instead of keeping it contained, boo. Get comfortable with that side of yourself and embrace it. Don't feel ashamed of it. Live free," Caria said.

"Yeah, I know what the word *free* means. I don't think I could be a hoe," Felicia said with a chuckle.

"This is some bullshit. This is the second time I've been referred as a hoe today! I know I'm a hoe. *Damn it*!"

Felicia stared at Caria until her rant was over, and both of them laughed. Caria insisted that Felicia get dressed. The day was turning out wonderful for her, and she wanted to make Felicia feel somewhat better than what she was feeling. Heading to the East Hampton mall, Caria tossed Felicia a plastic bag with purple buds inside it. Felicia examined the buds closely. It wasn't something she was used to smoking nor seeing, but she was ready for the journey this bud was bound to take her on. Her day was starting to shape up already as she broke the buds down smiling and bumping the crazy tunes. Caria was jamming too.

Felicia took a hit and filled her lungs with some of the most potent shit ever. The coughing frenzy began shortly after as she passed the purple devil over. She laid her head back on the headrest and let the spinning take control. For a moment she lost herself and thought, *What if I hadn't gotten married? What would my life be like? Could I really live the lifestyle Caria lives?* "Oh, shit! I'm stuck in my head!" she shouted out loud.

"Well, get the fuck out of there!" Caria replied. The car filled with laughter again as they pulled up to their destination. Caria noticed she chipped her nail closing the door, so plans changed to manicure and pedicure and then light shopping.

The day had been so relaxing for Felicia. It had been a long time since she was pampered, and hell she deserved it. Everything she had been through and was still somewhat going through was really starting to become a thorn in her side. As she had her feet rubbed to relieve the stress, she relaxed. She could breathe finally with peace of mind. She was thinking of Ron, the new job, and her new crush. A smile crossed her face when she thought of him, and for a few seconds the temperature seemed like it raised as beads of sweat trickled down her stomach.

"Enjoying the foot rub, darling?" Caria said startling Felicia back to reality.

"Yes, I am, boo. I also have a confession that I need to get off my chest. I really love your life, Caria. You're free to do whatever you want and have whomever you want, and the beauty of it is you don't have to explain *shit* to anybody. I bet your sex is fucking awesome too! I'm sorry, but there's no other term for what you look like you're capable of in bed. My apologies if you had to hear it like this, but I've been controlling myself long enough. Today is the day I start my change." Felicia finished her speech and smiled looking at Caria. She felt butterflies in her stomach. Her palms began to sweat as her heart thumped hard in her chest. Caria blushed at the compliments Felicia was giving her. Caria felt that was the green light to have Felicia if she wanted her, but Caria had a plan to take it slow.

"Boo, I promise you it isn't all that," Caria said sounding unconvincing. "You're beautiful; I mean have you looked at yourself, Felicia? I mean really looked at yourself? I would love to fuck and love the shit out of you, if you were into women. Those legs and that ass are plump, and you have the softest fucking skin I've ever felt. I love me, a beautiful mixed woman; but honestly, boo, I don't think you're ready for what I'm into, baby. You're still so innocent, and I don't want to scare you away from me, Felicia."

Felicia was done being the good girl. She wanted the bad boy. She wanted to be the bad girl.

Her body craved for the sexual aggression that Derek gave her. She wanted the chains and the cuffs along with the whips and blindfolds.

"How does it feel?" Felicia asked.

"What?"

"How does girl on girl feel?" Felicia replied.

Caria choked on her Sprite. "Umm, it feels good if you know what you're doing," Caria replied trying to clear her throat.

"Could you teach me?" Felicia asked.

"Umm, I could, but the timing would have to be right, and could we not have this conversation right now, Felicia? You're making me very horny, and all I can think of right now is ripping your clothes off," Caria replied to Felicia hoping that would end the conversation.

They both chuckled. Leaving the restaurant Caria and Felicia headed straight home. The time seemed like it caught up with the girls fast, and it was almost time for Caria to head to the club. She had just enough time to put the finishing touches of makeup on Felicia's face, and the girls were heading right back out the door to start the evening at the S&M.

Once inside the club Caria headed to the bar so she could get set up for the night. This was the first time Felicia had been inside the S&M when it was empty. She could walk around the club and get the feel of this place with no interruptions.

"The energy in this place is crazy, Caria! It's all sex whether it's filled with people or not," Felicia said as she stood in the middle of the dance floor laughing. Caria stared at Felicia from the bar as the disco lights flashed across Felicia's face. Caria knew right then that she had found her soul mate, but she was married; and although Felicia and Ron's marriage seemed like it was on a downward spiral, Caria wanted nothing to do with Felicia until she was single.

As Caria bit her lip still staring at Felicia, she knew she was known for many things, but breaking up homes was something she had never partaken in whether the home was happy or not. The DJ started with an opener for the working girls as they entered the building and continued the setup. Felicia watched the girls in their sexy outfits and heels as she walked over to the bar where Caria was waiting for her with the first shot of the night.

"Here. On three, toss it back," Caria said.

"Wait! What the hell am I tossing back?" Felicia asked laughing.

"Do you trust me?" Caria said as she smiled at Felicia. Felicia stood there like a deer in headlights as Caria waited for a response.

"I uh...I believe I do," Felicia replied.

"I need a straight yes or no answer, baby girl, and it's not that hard of a question. Either you trust me or you don't, so which is it?" Caria's tone remained calm, and she kept a smile on her face the whole time.

Felicia wasn't sure if this was a test for their relationship or not, but one thing was for sure, she wasn't ready to lose Caria just yet. Caria was the only person helping her progress from what happened. She was her only source of communication, and Felicia knew she trusted Caria with every bone in her body, but she wasn't sure why Caria needed to hear these words right now.

Felicia stood next to the bar for a few seconds and then replied, "Yes, Caria, I trust you. You've been an awesome and very supportive friend, and I love you for forcing this relationship on me."

The girls laughed and counted to three. The shots of 151 burned all the way down, and the night was just beginning. The club started filling up with people with their sexy leather suits and skintight corsets. Felicia remained close to Caria throughout the night, but that wasn't good enough for Felicia's reminiscent scenes in her head. Felicia kept thinking about the mini masturbation session that went on the last time she was in this club. Leaning over the bar Felicia yelled at Caria, "So where is the boss?"

Caria shrugged her shoulders; they hadn't seen Mr. Werth since the doors opened to the crowd.

Caria wasn't worried about seeing the boss. She was only interested in getting money, and that's exactly what she was getting working at the bar. Caria's outfit was bringing in money galore. Her tiny waist revealed a rose vine going down her body, and the short leather skirt complimented her booty as it hugged it just right with her black and silver belly shirt. Caria was one of the sexy dominant bartenders in the city, and she had Felicia's full attention as she watched Caria walk through the bar as if she owned it.

The shots of alcohol simmered through Felicia's system as she watched Caria. She was in love with her confidence and how she walked through life without fear. It was sexy and very attractive to everyone in the club; she even had Mr. Werth's attention as he watched her from his office monitors. No one had a clue that Derrell had been in his office watching since the crew had arrived. As the cameras rotated through the club, Derrell noticed that Felicia had returned. *So sweet and innocent*, he thought. *What the hell is this girl doing back in my club? She isn't ready to accept what this place has to offer*, he thought to himself. *She freaked out over a little pussy play that we had. She was so concerned with everyone watching she couldn't focus on the feeling, and her orgasms had to be forced.* Derrell mumbled out loud, "I don't fuck with babies; therefore, I shouldn't allow baby-ass women in my club!" He stormed out of his office heading down to join the rest of his crew. He planned to run Felicia off, but as he neared her, her smile seemed like it taunted him. He couldn't help but feel some type of way about her.

The feeling she struck in him was not the same feeling he felt for Caria. He slowed his pace as he got closer to Felicia, walking around the crowd watching her every move. Derrell was smitten by her. She was not normal in this scenery. She stuck out like a sore thumb, and it was driving him crazy.

In that moment as he watched Felicia and Caria together laughing and drinking, he figured he would get to know both of them, but the timing had to be right. Instead of cornering Felicia he decided to go with the regularly served dessert tonight. One of the cage dancer girls would have to do, but deep down Mr. Werth knew his appetite wouldn't be satisfied; however, it would have to work. He still had to fill Caria out because she would be the one in question. She was experienced in this atmosphere, and she wasn't gullible like her friend. Caria was far from being a dummy and nowhere near a virgin to life like Felicia. *Whom would I conquer first?* he thought to himself while watching the girls from afar. Both of them were beautiful, and both of them made his dick harder than life itself.

Derrell continued the night with the cage dancer fucking her in chains as he pictured Caria's body with Felicia's face, split images of the two women he craved for the most that night flashing back and forth. Derrell decided to stay out of sight tonight, for he was uncertain if Caria had mentioned him to Felicia or if Felicia had told Caria about him and the pussy play they had in the hallway a few nights back. He continued to watch the girls as he continued to fuck the cage dancer senseless.

The night went on until closing hours. When everything was finished Caria dropped Felicia off at home where she assumed her husband would be, but from the looks of the house, no one had been home since they left earlier that day. It was four o'clock in the morning, and Ron wasn't home yet. Felicia paid it no mind. She figured their marriage had run its course, and she was no longer interested in fighting for a bland marriage when she was craving spices.

"I've decided, Caria, tomorrow I'm heading downtown and I'm filing for a divorce."

"Are you sure, honey? He could be working late or out clearing his mind," Caria replied.

"Yes, I am. We've been unhappy for quite some time now, and I honestly think the only reason we've been hanging on this long is because of the kids," Felicia replied.

"I'm sorry, boo."

"For what? You're not the reason my marriage isn't working out. My cousins are doing good, and our son is doing good. I think it's the best thing for us. I'd rather leave than grow to resent him because we're forcing something that should have ended years ago," Felicia responded.

They sat in silence, and Felicia's thoughts had become finalized at that moment. She knew that it was going to happen eventually, but to hear herself say it out loud for the first time settled her mind; however, her heart was shattering into a million pieces. *I would file for a divorce, and Ron would be moving out, and we would go on with our lives,* she thought to herself with tears streaming down her face.

"Look, Felicia. Maybe you should see a counselor because looking at you, it doesn't seem like you're ready to give up on your husband," Caria said.

"I don't know how to make him happy anymore, Caria, and I'm not satisfied either. I don't want to keep flirting and messing with other people behind his back. He deserves better, someone who's going to be satisfied with pizza and movie night until they fall asleep in each other's arms you know," Felicia replied.

"Girl, you have what most of these hoes are craving for," Caria said. They both laughed at the comment Caria had just made. "You'll figure it out, Felicia. Just don't go making moves on uncertainty because that shit will fuck you up more than anything, love. Just think on it, and if you're still feeling having a divorce after you've spoken to your husband about everything, I'll be here to support your decision, love."

Felicia sat in silence for a few more seconds before agreeing with Caria. She got out of the car and headed to her door.

Meanwhile in prison things were running about the same for Derek. Not much had changed in those few months he was out. It was almost like returning home without any women involved. It had been eight months since Derek returned back to prison, and in eight months his brother hadn't been there to see him. Deangelo was disgusted by Derek's actions toward a friend they both knew since high school. Derek had written to his brother several times since his return, but Deangelo's silence remained. He owed Derek nothing but being the warden of the prison he knew he couldn't continue ignoring his prisoners if he wanted to remain the boss around De'Shjine.

"About time you sent for me. Here I thought the rumors around the yard were true! Are you that mad at your baby brother?" Derek asked with sarcasm.

"Derek, just because we're family, man, doesn't mean you get any special treatment from me! I'm going to start treating you like every other inmate in this prison, boy, so you can stop with all the letters of request. Your free ride is over, nigga! You go learn to take responsibility for your actions and your life. *I'm done*!" Deangelo shouted.

Derek sat in silence for a few minutes before it turned into a small chuckle. "You say take responsibility for my actions. It's funny you say that because, nigga, I'm the only reason you are still alive in this motherfucker. Nigga, there's a target on your head. There has been one since I got out of this motherfucker, you bitch-ass nigga, and this is how you want to thank me? *Fuck you*!" Derek replied as he came to a stand walking toward the door.

"What the fuck are you talking about, Derek? A target on me for what? I'm not the criminal. That's your department, *fool*!" Deangelo's voice rose with hostility.

"*Nigga*, you might not be a criminal, but you are stupid as fuck. You and that dumb-ass dick of yours always letting that raggedy motherfucker think for you," Derek replied with sarcasm.

"Once again, Derek, I have no fucking clue as to what you're talking about."

"You're fucking Diablo's wife, nigga; and he got pictures to prove it, big brother. He's shown the whole crew the pictures of big bruh," Derek said with a smirk on his face. "The way you tied that hoe in knots with that rope, I must admit that was some sexy shit, bruh man. I mean I can't even manage knots like that. Then you were beating it from the back with your hand on her throat," Derek said still smiling, licking his lips as he continued to explain what the pictures showed. "My favorite one was how you folded that bitch up and fucked the shit out of her, bruh. Her facial expressions told the whole story, bruh man, and that shit was priceless." Derek groped himself still smiling at Deangelo.

As Derek sat back down in his seat laughing, he could tell Deangelo was just figuring out whom the hell he was talking about, and everything that had been happening made sense. The vehicle explosion in the parking lot, the two officers killed the night of the Halloween party that he didn't show up for—it was all starting to come together, and by the expression he held on his face, Derek knew then that he couldn't just write him off so easy. One thing Derek did have around his brother's prison was pull; anything he needed or could possibly want, Derek could get it, so that made him the man around De'Shjine.

After Derek left the office, he joined the other inmates in the cafeteria leaving his brother with a lot of newfound information to take into consideration. Deangelo knew his brother was a well-respected inmate, and this made things difficult because Deangelo wasn't ready to forgive Derek for what he did to Felicia, but he wasn't ready to die for fucking one of the mafia's bitches. Deangelo was at a crossroad, and Derek gave him until the end of the day to think about his proposal, either get on board on giving him his freedom and lead way back or sleep with the fishes. Upset that he had gotten himself in such a dilemma, Deangelo knew the better option would be with his brother, but he was having a hard time getting over the fact that he would be rewarding his brother for a fucked-up crime.

"Get up, inmate, and follow me," the guard said as she walked past him in her skintight uniform.

"*Hmmm*, I see something new has come to De'Shjine while I was gone," Derek replied as he smiled at the female guard.

The officer turned and gestured a smile to the inmate.

"Damn, Ma! You are fine as hell. What's a woman like you doing in a place like this, baby?" Derek asked trying to spark a conversation between the two as they walked down the hall.

"Quiet, inmate." She walked slowly in front of him. Derek had no argument with her. He just focused on the globe-like ass that was taunting him.

"Have a seat, and the warden will be with you shortly," the guard said as she walked back to the entry of the library.

"So, baby, you got a name?" Derek asked.

"Yes, I do," she responded but didn't say.

"Do you want to tell me what it is, baby?" Derek responded to her dry reply.

"Derek, don't worry about my name. Just know that I know you and I know what you're capable of, okay? I won't be getting involved with you like the last female officer you strangled out," the guard replied.

"Damn, I just asked you your fucking name, not for you to come and serve my dick after we are down, stuck-up bitch."

"Derek, watch your mouth," Deangelo said as he entered the library. "So here's all the stuff you were asking for, and as for the other shit, I'm going to need like a week to get it approved, and then we can go from there."

"That's all good and everything, but I only need one more favor from you, brother. I must warn you. You're not going to like it, not one bit," Derek said as he sat in silence grinning at Deangelo.

From the smile Derek held on his face, Deangelo knew it wasn't going to be easy whatever it was Derek was about to ask of him.

"What the fuck do you need, Derek? It had better not be anything stupid or crazy!" Deangelo replied.

Derek filled the room with laughter and responded, "It's both, bruh, stupid and crazy!"

With the sound of regret in his tone, Deangelo asked, "What is it, Derek?"

"*Awww*, don't be like that, bruh. It's a plan for my first-step program." Derek laughed again.

"What the fuck is it, Derek?!"

"Okay, bruh, I need you to mail a visitor form to Felicia so she can come see me," Derek replied.

Stunned that Derek was even talking about Felicia, Deangelo stood in silence hoping Derek was joking.

"Did you hear me, bruh? I need you to get that done for me, and once she's on the visiting shit, you can live scathe-free, and it comes with benefits," Derek responded.

"What benefits?"

"You can continue fucking ol' girl," Derek responded.

"Hold on. What does Felicia have to do with me being off the hook from Diablo? I don't see how that's a bargain," Deangelo said with concern.

"Dude, you shouldn't be worried about anybody but yourself. After all you're the one who's going to die if that bitch doesn't come and see me, and I do mean soon!" Derek replied.

"I can't, Derek. I need to know what the hell Felicia has to do with this?"

"*Dammit, bruh*! Why do you have a fucking conscience now? Just take the fucking deal and run with it," Derek demanded.

"*Fuck no, nigga*! You go tell me what the fuck Felicia has to do with this."

Derek smirked. "She's going to be a great server for us," Derek said.

"*Us? Who the fuck is us, Derek*?!" Deangelo asked sounding almost like he was begging for more information.

"Well, since you need to know, big brother, the mafia dude has the hots for Ms. Felicia."

"Wait. How does Diablo know Felicia, Derek?"

"Let's see. How can I explain this without making it complicated? Felicia's mother is Diablo's mother's go-to girl. She has been for quite some time now," Derek replied.

"Derek, you're not about to sit here and tell me that Sandy is tied up with them people. They're nothing but drug dealers and murderers and shit like that!" Deangelo shouted in rage.

"Call them whatever the fuck you want, bruh. I just know that nigga's family is paid and has been paid for a long ass time now; and Sandy, bruh, she has been in the game before she even decided to give birth, bruh. I'm talking before Diablo was born. That's how long she has been in the game with that nigga's family," Derek replied with a straight face this time.

"Wait. Why is he willing to work with you after what you did to Felicia? I mean if he's so sweet on her and all?" Deangelo replied out of confusion. "It just doesn't make any sense to me, Derek."

"D, listen. What I am about to tell you might piss you off, but I don't give a fuck because that's just who I am." He laughed. "The shit with Felicia was a setup for Diablo. He wanted me to get close to Felicia and find a way into her head, and that's exactly what I did," Derek responded.

"How is raping a woman in the gym and beating her half to death getting close to her?" Deangelo asked with his face frowned.

"Sandy is trying to get out of the agreement that the mafia mom has set up, so with that being said, I had a job to do and I did it, which is another reason you still got your life, nigga. So if I were you, I would stop asking so many fucking questions and just get your part done," Derek replied as he turned in the direction of the guard checking her out again. "What happened to Felicia was nothing personal for me. It was just business, but I must admit that shit was good. That bitch got some wet, bruh. It was tight like homegirl's pants over there, and it smelled good. I honestly had a ball beating that shit open again."

"You're sick, Derek! How the fuck could you do that to your own friend?" Deangelo said as he dropped his head.

"Man, shut the fuck up. That bitch wasn't a friend of mine. She fucked me and then left me for some lame-ass nigga that she calls her husband. That bitch wasn't thinking about me and my feelings, so fuck her and her feelings!" Derek came to a stand and started out of the library. "D, I know this isn't your scene, my nigga; but at the end of the day, nobody goes to the grave clean, my nigga. Your time is now, bruh. Either die for that bitch or get her the fuck up here. I'm done talking," he replied to Deangelo. "I'm ready, big booty. Lead the way." He smiled at the guard waiting for her to walk in front of him so he could enjoy the view again.

Sitting in his cell Derek thought about Felicia and the way he did her. Although he was putting on a front in front of his brother, Derek was really hurting deep down from hurting Felicia, but he had a choice to make. He could lose his brother, or he could demolish the love he had for Felicia.

Derek lived by one rule in life, and that was family above any other, and his brother was the last of his family. He really needed Deangelo to get those forms to Felicia and get her on the visitors' list before the week was over. He paced back and forth hoping Deangelo would do what he was asking of him, but his gut felt something totally different.

Deangelo was placed in a situation where he had to choose between his life and an old friend's. He wasn't quite sure what was going to happen to Felicia, but he knew he didn't want to be the reason something bad would happen to her. It had been years since Deangelo and Felicia had seen or heard from each other, but Deangelo had to think of a way to get in touch with Felicia without it feeling weird. Deangelo sent a message to her on Facebook letting her know that it was very important that they meet to speak about his brother's prison situation.

Deangelo wasn't sure if Felicia would respond to his message. He thought to himself, *Why the hell would she respond to this nigga after he raped her and damn near succeeded in killing her?* To his surprise the Messenger lit up with one new message.

"I'm not sure if this is a sick joke, D, but it's not funny! I don't want to hear what you have to say about your brother," Felicia replied to his message.

"Hey, Felicia, please hear me out. I just need to speak with you in person. I've gotten myself into some shit, and the only person who can help me is you. Please don't turn your back on me, girl," Deangelo responded.

"What the hell? If I meet you anywhere, it's going to be out in the open, and I won't be alone," Felicia replied.

"That's fine, Felicia, and to make it better you can even pick the place wherever you want."

"*Great*! You can meet me at the S&M downtown tomorrow night. That's the only time I'll be able to see you. I have a busy week ahead of me," Felicia replied.

"Sweet. I'll see you there, Felicia. Thanks, lady. I owe you one," Deangelo replied feeling complete with his mission.

As Felicia sat in front of her computer, she wondered what the hell Derek and Deangelo wanted and why it was so important for them to have to talk in person. She hadn't seen nor heard from Deangelo, not even after what Derek did to her. Felicia was really starting to wreck her mind over it. "Let me stop thinking about this shit before my brain explodes," she said as she rolled her blunt and took it to the face.

Meanwhile back in prison Derek was setting up deals when Diablo approached him in the yard.

"What's up, homie? Is everything in order yet?"

"It's in process, Diablo. I spoke with my brother about mailing Felicia the visitor form for you, but the only thing about it is she's going to be visiting me first. Then I'll explain to her what's going on, and then the next will be a personal private visit for you, if that's cool with you," Derek replied.

"That's great. I love the way you set shit up, boy. You're a fucking soldier, and you get the job *done*! I need more of you in my squad," Diablo responded with a smirk on his face.

"Yeah, I know. I just need you to keep in mind that I'm only doing this for my brother, Diablo. I'm sorry he fucked your wife and everything. He is just that kind of stupid, educated but still stupid!" Derek replied as the crew joined together laughing.

"Honestly that bitch was on her way out the door anyway. She was fucking niggas before I was locked up."

"If that's true, why put my brother through this bullshit for an unloyal-ass bitch?" Derek asked with a disgruntled tone.

"We needed somebody to get to Felicia. You think I'm stupid? We've been setting this shit up for a while, and your brother was just one of the keys that fit into my plans perfectly. You both know Felicia, and that's what I needed. You know how long I've been waiting for that girl to grow up. I mean Sandy did her thing when she had both of her daughters, but there's just something about Felicia and that pretty-ass skin. She's always been soft, and I've always had eyes for her; but with the way our bloodline is set up, Italians stay with Italians, and blacks stay with blacks. But something happened when she was born, and that rule just never made sense to me. Feel me?" Diablo explained.

Derek replied, "Hell, yeah! I feel you, but that was also a long time ago, dude. You're not that much older than us, which means you grew up when the times were changing; so if I had to play chess with you, I would say you've had your fair share of brown sugar. You just never settled down with one because of your mother. She must be the one who comes from a different time, and she would never understand your point of view on why you love brown sugar. Am I close?"

"You know you're smart ass, fuck boy, and that's why you're the only reason your brother is still alive and breathing. I respect you although we'll never be equals. I need you to know that I respect you and your mind frame because you're nothing like these other niggas in here. Hell, you aren't even like your brother, paisan. You're smarter than him. If we were playing chess, I would say the only reason you came to prison is so you could protect your bitch-ass brother because he isn't man enough to run a prison of this magnitude. If you weren't his right-hand man helping him and keeping the inmates in order, that motherfucker would have been lunch meat!" Diablo said with a clenched jaw. "He doesn't respect you like he should, paisan. I even sense jealousy when you're around each other."

"I'm not sure what the fuck you're talking about, my brother. He doesn't have a reason to be jealous of me. As for me being locked up, well, that's another story, and I'm no storyteller; but he is getting shit together, so we should be hearing from Felicia soon," Derek replied changing the subject because he was getting irritated with Diablo but also trying to maintain his composure.

Diablo could sense that he was getting under Derek's skin by talking about his brother, and Derek knew the moves of chess very well. The smartest move to make now was to change the subject so his blood could cool down from the intense conversation that had taken place.

Derek focused on the rest of the yard, while Diablo continued to talk out the side of his neck. The more he talked, the more Derek focused his attention on the basketball court as the dudes played hard against each other. After a few moments Diablo ended the conversation he was having with himself and walked off with his squad following three steps behind.

As the fellas all walked away, Derek thought to himself about the stuff Diablo had just said to him involving his brother. Was Diablo noticing something that he had never paid any attention to, or was Diablo really trying to get into his head to turn him against the only family he had left? Not sure on what to believe, Derek decided to shake that shit out of his head and worry about the meeting that Deangelo and Felicia had coming up.

"Damn, man, I hope that nigga get that bitch to agree to get her ass up here so I can fill her in on what's going on," he said to himself as he walked back toward the building for head count.

Felicia waited patiently as she watched the entrance doors for Deangelo to arrive at the club. It was supposed to be a special night for her because it was time to meet with Mr. Werth and convince him to give her a job working for his club. While she waited she wondered how things would go with Deangelo and why it was so important that they meet with each other. Meanwhile, Deangelo had been waiting in line for almost an hour trying to get inside the S&M. As he stood looking at everyone, it didn't take him long to figure out what kind of club this was, not to mention he was the only one in line overdressed.

There had been no sign of Mr. Werth as Felicia scanned the club looking for a handsomely well-dressed man in a suit; however, looking back toward the entrance, she saw Deangelo finally walking into the building.

"Hey, D! D!" Felicia shouted his name from the bar.

When his eyes locked with Felicia's, all those high school memories flooded his mind. *Felicia has always been a sight for sore eyes*, Deangelo thought to himself as he greeted Felicia with a warm smile.

"Hey, beautiful, how have you been?" Deangelo asked with a hug.

"I'm fine. I've been fine, and you?"

"Oh, you know it's good, but it could always be better," Deangelo replied making his facial expression a little more serious.

"So to make a long story short, what is this about?"

"Well, I thought we could speak somewhere private, Felicia."

"Why would we do that?"

"I just figured the shit I have to share with you is not for public ears, Felicia," Deangelo responded with a straight gaze.

"I'm not hearing that. Whatever you have to say to me, you can say it now; otherwise, I'm going to be on my way."

"Look, Felicia. I'm not trying to play games with you, girl! I have some important shit to talk to you about, and if you're too fucking busy to hear me out, then someone is going to *die*! I'm not sure whom it is; but for now let's just say it's not looking too good for you, me, or your *mother*!" Deangelo shouted bringing attention to himself and Felicia.

"*Shhhh*!" Felicia responded to his yelling. She turned toward the crowd and smiled gesturing for people to mind their business. "What the fuck does my mother have to do with anything, Deangelo?"

"Felicia, please listen to me. It's a lot of bullshit going on, and it's a lot deeper than we both know, but Derek has—"

"*What the fuck has Derek got to do with anything*?!" Felicia shouted interrupting Deangelo.

"Could I finish, Felicia?"

"Hell, no. I don't understand what that sick fuck got to do with me or my mom, Deangelo!"

"*Shut the fuck up, Felicia, please*! This is not a fucking game. If we don't sit down soon and talk like adults, someone is going to die. If we don't and someone does get hurt, I hope you'll be fine living with their blood on your hands!" Deangelo dropped his head and headed for the exit.

"Wait, D. *Wait*!" Felicia shouted.

"*What*?!" Deangelo turned. "I don't have time for this. I can barely hear you in this place, and with the way everyone is dressed, I'm feeling a little uncomfortable because I'm clearly wearing too much material," Deangelo replied breaking the tension between the two as he joked at the leathery suits and masked people freaking all over each other.

Felicia chuckled as she grabbed Deangelo's hand and wrote her number on his palm. "Call me tomorrow. Maybe we can meet at the coffee shop on Delphis and Main. It's right around the corner from my place. We can talk there without any interruptions."

"Please don't play me, Felicia. This shit really has me spooked," Deangelo replied as he looked around the club once more. "Girl, you really are into some wild shit. I have to get going because this place is freaking me out," Deangelo said with a smirk.

Felicia laughed. She could tell that Deangelo was really out of his comfort zone. "I'll be there in the morning. Just call me, and I promise to have on more when we meet tomorrow," Felicia responded.

"By the way, you do look incredibly sexy," Deangelo replied to Felicia's naked joke.

Deangelo walked away as Felicia stood in the doorway watching him until he disappeared into the shadows of the night. Returning back to the bar, Felicia noticed Caria was gone from her post. She looked around on the dance floor, and there was no sign of Caria. Felicia walked through the club searching the VIP section and the restrooms. There was still no sign of her. She noticed a hidden stairwell around from the ladies' restrooms. The air from the hall blew the curtains open and revealed that there was a whole other side to the club.

Blue lights flashed across her face as she proceeded up the stairwell. Once she reached the top level, she saw doors on each side while women stood naked in the halls kissing and rubbing each other. Walking by the doorways she saw different colors of lights. Felicia caught on fast that each room had a special theme to it. As she peeked into the green room, a small crowd of people stood around watching couples having sex with each other. Walking to the next flashing color, Felicia found herself looking at people experimenting with all types of toys. People were engaging with cock rings, vibrators, dildos, and oils. As she continued to glance through the color blue, she noticed men having sex with fake pussies, while women sat at their feet ready to catch the men's load when the time came.

A little confused by what she was seeing, she continued down the hall looking for Caria until she came across the red room where it seemed like anything went. The people were trying all types of items and sex positions to get that nut off. It was the bittersweet color of pain and pleasure after she saw the woman chained to the bed with nipple clamps, while her man covered in black leather lubed up some big beads and put them in her asshole. She was intrigued, but she wasn't ready for it yet. As she continued her journey down the hall, she thought to herself, *This is out of my league. What the hell would make people want to get into this crazy shit?* She chuckled down the hall to herself. She was definitely far away from home as she traveled the hallway to freak fest. Then at the end of the hall was a black room. No colors were flashing, no people were gathering around to see strange couples together, and nobody was placing items in other people's bootyholes, just black silk sheets with a candle burning. Walking in the room she looked around. There were no cuffs or chains connected to the bed. This room seemed like it was designed for her and her husband. She laughed at the thought.

"I don't believe you were invited up here," the voice said, startling her.

When she turned in the direction of the voice, she was grabbed by her hair.

"I don't believe I asked you to look at me either," the stranger said.

"Look. I'm just up here looking for my friend Caria. She works here, okay?"

"Still no reason for you to go snooping through people's things," he replied with a stern tone.

"I was just leaving. If you let me go, I can leave right now."

"Now why would I let you go? You seemed so curious when you were walking down the halls poking your nose where it didn't belong. If you ask me, from where I'm standing, it seemed like you were choosing; and guess what, my little wallflower. You picked the right color because there is nothing about you that screams experienced!" the voice snarled in her ear as he gripped her hair tighter.

"*Excuse me*!" Pissed off by the insult, she turned toward him not caring about him pulling her hair. "*You*!" Her eyes lit up. "You're my masked man. I mean you're the masked man I saw the last time I was here."

He stood in silence not saying a word, but she could tell he was happy to see her. She could feel him breathing on her skin as he rubbed his face through her hair. His hands were all over her body and then pulled her hair again bringing her head back while he leaned in to greet her with his lips. He continued to rub the leather mask on her face. The more this man touched her, the more her body craved for excitement.

Although he never confirmed he was her masked man, something told her deep down it was him.

His touch was so familiar, and his insults were more brutal but still on point about her life. She let herself get lost in his scent again. If any man could pull off 1 million cologne and leather, it would be this man with his slender build.

"Since we're in the black room, I would like to try something. That's if you're not afraid," the masked man said.

She looked at him without even noticing her facial expression was changing.

"Judging from the smile I can tell you're excited to see me again," he said as he continued to rub all over her body. "I'm going to try something, so close your eyes."

He locked his fingers around her fingers. Then she felt his tongue twirling around her pinkie finger, and he walked off and left her standing there. "Don't open your eyes until I say you can," he said to her once more. Her heart thumped hard in her throat, but she refused to turn away this time. She was curious about him and everything he had to offer or at least wanted to teach her. Derrell began rubbing what felt like a rope around her waist and then moving the rope around her ass.

"Put your hands above your head and keep them there."

She did exactly what she was told this time. She didn't want him to think she was still afraid of him although she was pretty sure he could see her heart beating out the side of her neck. He placed a kiss on her stomach as she felt the ropes tighten around her wrist. How was she so distracted that she didn't feel the ropes until he tightened them? She'd lost herself in him, and she enjoyed every moment of it. As she hung on the ropes, he pulled her bottoms off her lower half. A few moments after undressing her, her body began to tingle.

"I've always liked the feather. It causes women to go crazy if touched correctly. I use these for my pleasure, not yours."

She didn't quite understand what that meant. All she knew was whatever it was he was doing was turning her on. She didn't want to resist anymore. She could feel her pussy throbbing to where it was more pain than pleasure. All she wanted was for him to stuff his dick inside her and ease the feeling he was causing. She needed to be set free. Then she felt his lips kissing her again. Each kiss was soft and moist, trailing from her stomach down to her jungle of lust. His tongue caressed her clitoris so slowly, and at that moment she felt herself building up to an orgasm; but every time she neared her release, he would stop causing an even more agonizing pain of sexual tension.

She wanted to cum, and she wanted to do it in his mouth. She wanted him to suck her sweet nectar out of her while she came so hard on his soft lips, but he obviously wanted to play with her. Sticking his fingers inside her, she felt herself instantly squirt as soft moans escaped her mouth. He nibbled on her nipples intensifying the feeling. Her pussy was now dripping wet from the excitement. She could tell he was just as ready from the bulge in his suit. The more he rubbed against her, the harder he felt.

"If you're going to fuck me, please let's get started because I can't take it anymore." She sighed hanging on the ropes that he tied her to.

He placed a finger over her mouth for her to quiet down. Then she felt his fingers intrude her honey hovel again pushing them in and out and then rotating in different directions.

"I can feel you clenching your pussy, baby girl. Your walls are so smooth, and it's tight like a virgin which means I was right when I met you. You've been neglected, huh, baby girl? I'm not sure if you can handle the size that I have for you tonight," Derrell said as he sucked the wetness from his fingers tasting her and staring at her naked physique.

"Please I want you inside of me. Please make me cum like before."

"I like when you beg me for my dick, baby. It's very sexy to have a woman beg me for once. I've never had the chance to experience that one before. Usually these chicks are begging me to stop, and here you are begging me to start." Derrell felt good about how the evening was going as he smiled at her with her eyes still closed.

He placed his fingers back into her wet world and continued finger-fucking her driving her body crazy. Her breathing became heavy as she moaned out. Her pussy was screaming for more pleasure, but he insisted on teasing her.

"I would really enjoy it if you cut me down and fucked me lifeless."

"I don't want you lifeless, just weak, baby, so weak and sore that you won't be able to move for three days, baby girl."

She swallowed hard, and before she could utter another word, his mouth was on her pussy sucking and licking as her body trembled out of control. The pleasure was on max, and she was so ready to cum, but he wasn't giving her body that extra oomph it was crying for. "*Please*, Derrell, make me cum," she moaned.

"No, baby, it's not time, nor do I believe you deserve it," Derrell replied.

"*Why*?!" she shouted, becoming angry.

"Because, baby girl, you've been bad. You were never invited upstairs to play. Like I said you need to have an invitation. People with invitations can cum all night long, but bad girls get the torture part of the sex when they don't listen," Derrell responded to Felicia who had just been shocked by the response she had just gotten and opened her eyes.

Derrell continued to tease her with vibrators and feathers as she hung there lost for words. Fed up with the sexual torment, she figured she would focus on having an orgasm as she bit her lip.

Derrell noticed her change of mood as she became more relaxed.

"See you're so hardheaded. You can't even follow simple rules, just like a child, only in it to get what you want! You're such a selfish individual, Ms. Felicia. You don t care about other's feelings or needs at all, do you?"

"I do care about your needs. That's why I asked you to fuck me!" Felicia shouted.

"No, I don't want to fuck you tonight, but I will hit you now."

"*What*?"

Smack! Her ass stung from the paddle he'd just hit her with. "Now you can go, and don't return until you learn some manners or at least receive an invitation," Derrell replied as he walked out of the room leaving her with her thoughts about the evening.

She hung on the ropes sexually frustrated and confused. She couldn't figure out what the hell she did wrong. Why would he call me selfish and then hit me? The motherfucker just left me. How the hell did he expect me to get free? The thoughts became unbearable. She was embarrassed and really rethinking about getting hired at this place. How could she work with such a jackass like Derrell?

"How the fuck do I get down?"

"*Wow, Felicia*!"

"Caria, is that you? Please get me down!"

Caria walked around Felicia taking in the view while laughing.

"What the hell are you doing up here, Felicia?"

"First, I want you to know that this is all your fault. Second, please stop laughing because it's hurting my feelings. And, third, get me the hell down because this whole fucking night has been complete bullshit!" Felicia shouted.

"Felicia, how the hell is this my fault? I didn't even know about this place. I was doing my walk-through training for other spots of the club, and I ran into Mr. Werth telling me a girl needed my assistance on the second level in the black room. I was thinking a waitress dropped bottles, but clearly you could see I was just as surprised as you when I saw it was you, here, completely naked, tied up," Caria replied still chuckling.

"I was looking for you by the VIP section, okay? I saw the curtain. Then the wind blew, and I saw steps and lights, and here I am. Please get me down now, Caria!"

"I notice you keep avoiding the question, so I'll just get detailed. Who tied you up and undressed you, Felicia?"

"A guy I thought I liked, but he's an asshole, so never mind him. I just want to get down so I can go home."

"So you met a stranger, then you let him tie you up after undressing you, and then he just left you? Is that what you're telling me, Felicia?"

"*Oh my god*! This is crazy. Just get these damn ropes off of me so I can leave this fucking place! I've never been so humiliated in my life. I'm never coming back to this shit hole!"

Caria chuckled some more.

"Well, honey, I hate to break it to you, but when I did see Mr. Werth, he informed me that you could start your training tomorrow. So would you like for me to tell him never mind since you're never coming back in this shit hole?" Caria replied laughing.

"*Bitch*, it's not funny! I'm naked and cold, and my wrists are hurting from being tied up, and wait. Did you say I got the job? *But* wait. I never saw Mr. Werth. How could he give me a job and didn't even meet with me?"

"I told him you looked like me," Caria replied still laughing. After letting it sink in, Felicia began to jump up and down filled with excitement. She could now leave the airport and start her new journey. Caria stood back and took in the naked sight of Felicia once more as she became aroused from the curves of her best friend. Caria moved closer to her as if she was about to free her from the ropes, but instead she rubbed her hands from the center of her back down to Felicia's firm ass gripping each cheek as she looked into her soul.

"Caria, what are you doing?" Felicia asked with a trembling voice.

"I must admit something to you, Felicia. I've been crushing on you for quite a while now. Then I find you up here completely naked, in the area where anything goes. I can only assume that this is fate," Caria replied.

"Caria, you know I've never been with a woman."

"Don't worry, baby. I'll only do what you want me to do. So what would Felicia like me to do?" Caria asked. Unsure if Caria was joking, Felicia laughed it off as she looked at Caria. The room filled with silence as Caria stared at her with stern eyes biting her lip. Felicia could hear her heartbeat pounding. Caria was stirring up the same emotions that Derrell had just abandoned. New flame flared throughout the club downstairs, but in Felicia's head the music was right there in the room with them. She was horny, and she was very interested in Caria.

Caria rubbed her face across Felicia's soft supple breast as she watched. The touch was inviting for Felicia as Caria worked her way around her body placing soft kisses. Caria stood back undressing as Felicia hung on the ropes watching the show. Standing completely naked Caria walked toward Felicia and undid the ropes that were tightly wrapped around her wrists.

Rubbing the indents on Felicia's skin, Caria wondered why would the person tie the ropes so tight around Felicia's beautiful soft skin as she kissed each indent softly. After kissing her wrist Caria placed another kiss, but this time it was on the lips. Then she placed another kiss to break the ice and then another for dominance.

The last kiss was firm and aggressive as she set the mood to let Felicia know that she was in charge. Felicia accepted the invitation that Caria was sending to her. The kisses became deeper as the sighs became irresistible. Caria pushed her to the bed and kissed her from her ankle up to her knee until she was comfortable at her mid-thigh placing soft wet kisses and then diving into her love spell. Felicia moaned out from the pleasure as Caria continued to suck and lick her love pearl not holding back at all. She finally had her chance with Felicia, and she made up her mind that this would be the perfect time to devour her.

She placed two fingers inside her pussy as she continued to suck on her clitoris. Felicia's body seemed like it was changing seasons going from cold to hot to shivering and then hot again. Her eyes couldn't keep sight of what was going on, but her body recognized everything that Caria was doing to it as she slid her fingers in and out and sucked her clit harder.

"Caria! Shit, Caria!"

Felicia could hear Caria's name escaping her lips as Caria pleasured every ounce of her infatuation. She was coming over and over again. This was definitely something she had never felt, and here she was experiencing her first set of multiple orgasms with a woman. After her body gave all it could give, she opened her eyes to Caria crawling over her head and placing her pussy in her mouth. With the fact that Caria really liked her, Felicia wanted to satisfy her as well. She mimicked every move that Caria performed on her as she rode her face. It was something about the way she rotated her hips while grinding her pussy in her mouth that turned her on more.

She couldn't help but hold on to her soft round ass squeezing it as she sucked away at her clit. The more she dripped, the more Felicia wanted to taste her. She tasted like vanilla, and the smell of her body drove her crazy. She was incredible. She leaned over her head and began pulling away and then coming closer riding her face like it was a dick attached, so she placed two fingers in her wet pussy and sucked harder on her pearl. Caria's body became very still as she moaned out Felicia's name. Her dominance had left her, and she was folding. It was her time to make Caria her bitch. She finger-fucked her harder while twirling her tongue vigorously around her clit until her body exploded and she collapsed over her.

"Where the fuck did that come from?" Caria asked as she hovered over Felicia's head.

"It came from the mouth underneath you, love," Felicia replied as she continued to suck on Caria's love pearl gently.

"Oh, please stop. I can't take it anymore," Caria replied trying to roll her limp body over.

Both the girls filled the room with laughter as Caria tried getting up without falling. After a few moments of wobbles, Caria was able to walk over to the glass case that contained different lengths of dildos. She grabbed the one that she thought Felicia would be comfortable with. It wasn't too big, but it wasn't nowhere near small either. She walked back over to Felicia who was ready for her second serving of pleasure. Felicia opened her legs, and Caria went in face first attacking her clit with a vengeance as she penetrated her with the dildo.

They went on with each other unaware of Derrell watching them from his office screen with a rock-solid dick that he stroked smiling. Derrell was finally proud of Felicia for opening up to the foreign life of sexuality. He craved both of them, and to see them together so comfortable with each other, he had to figure out a way to get in the middle of them. Derrell buzzed downstairs to the bar to send up a cage girl. He needed to think while she sucked the stress and tension away.

A few minutes after her alarm clock sounded off, Felicia began to stretch and yawn getting out of the bed heading into the bathroom. Sitting on the toilet she flashed back to the mini episode of her and Caria and the time well spent last night. She couldn't believe that she just had a full-on steamy sex scene with a woman. Shaking her head she felt good about the decision she made.

Her morning seemed a lot brighter than usual, and then her phone rang.

"Hello."

"Hey, woman, did you forget about me?" Deangelo asked.

"*Oh, shit*! D, I'm brushing my teeth and heading out the door now," Felicia responded as she hung up the phone rushing to get this meeting done and over with.

She threw on a white beater and some jeans and headed out the door with the mouthwash still burning, while she gargled it around and spit it out once she arrived outside.

"Hello, sir, would you like to order anything?" the waiter asked.

"Yes, please. Coffee, black," Deangelo replied as he watched the door waiting for Felicia to arrive.

"Would that be all, sir?"

"Yes, for now, but there will be another person arriving shortly. Maybe you could come back when she gets here," Deangelo replied. As he sat waiting patiently for Felicia, he decided to work on his approach to start the conversation of dramatics. *How the hell am I going to convince this girl to go to this fucking prison to see this damn fool?* he thought out loud.

"Hey, what's up, D? My fault I'm late. I overslept, man. Last night was kind of wild for me," Felicia stated with a smirk on her face.

"Whom are you telling? You look like shit, Felicia," Deangelo replied. Felicia could only smile at the comment that was just sent her way. She enjoyed every bit of what she went through last night, but for the moment it wasn't up for discussion.

"So what's up, D? I believe we had enough of the small talk," she said as she smirked at him.

"Damn, straight to the point, huh?"

"Yes, there's no need to drag this out longer than we have to. We haven't seen each other in years, and you've never tried to reach out before, so I'm assuming this is something your brother is trying to set up. Am I right?" Felicia asked and patiently waited for a response.

"Here is your coffee, sir. Can I get you anything, ma'am?" the waiter asked, ready to take orders.

"No, the coffee is fine for now, love," Deangelo replied. The waiter walked off, and Deangelo was able to finish the conversation he was having before they were interrupted again. "Yes, Felicia, it is about my brother; but that's only a piece of the puzzle, love. Can you tell me anything about your mother's past? Like what she did for a living?"

"I don't understand. What the hell does my mother have to do with anything?"

"Look. I got to be honest with you. Your mother was into some crazy shit before she had you or even considered living the life that she's living now. I truly don't understand what she has to do with what's going on now, but like I said it's a bunch of crazy shit that I can't even fathom right now, Felicia."

"What the fuck are you talking about, D? My mother is a fucking counselor for teens. Always have been!"

"I'm sorry, boo, but your mom has been lying to you; and now I'm afraid we're both about to pay the price with our lives if your mom doesn't go see the people she used to work for back in the day, or you could come to the prison and see Derek. He's the only one who knows the whole backdrop to what's going on, and he's our only option right now."

"Please don't take this the wrong way, but you want me to go see a nigga who about killed me and, not only that, confessed to me that he stalked me for over a year after we went our separate ways?" Felicia responded.

"*Yes*," Deangelo replied.

"So fuck the fact the he raped me, right? Fuck the fact that he held a knife to my throat as he fucked me, right? Not only are you asking me to go see this asshole, but you're accusing my mother of doing some other shit!?" Felicia shouted.

"Excuse me, guys. I have other customers. Could you please keep it down?" the redheaded waiter said as she returned to their table.

"Sure, sorry for the outburst," Deangelo responded.

"I don't follow you, D. I'm sorry, but I'm going to say no. I don't believe the shit you're saying about my mother, and I don't believe the shit about us being killed. All this shit sounds like to me your brother is looking for a cut-down on his sentence, and he's not going to get it from me."

Felicia stood up from the table and began to walk away. Deangelo felt that he had given it his all, but he wasn't ready to die yet, so he stood up from the table and shouted at Felicia.

"*Bitch*! You may want to die, but I don't, so have your ass at that fucking prison to see my brother Friday at 8:00 a.m. If you're late it's a must that I let you know that I will be alerting the motherfuckers in the prison of your whereabouts and your mother's address! I'm not dying for you bitches!"

Felicia turned in disgust. "What the fuck, nigga?! Are you threatening me? I'll have your ass put to sleep if you keep talking to me like you don't have any damn sense!" Felicia shouted again.

"*Excuse me*! But I'm going to have to ask you two to leave my shop!" the waiter shouted at both of them.

Deangelo smiled at the waiter and then turned toward Felicia. "Bitch, I'm sure you'll probably be using the resources from your mother."

"Once again, bitch, my mother doesn't have shit to do with what the fuck you're spitting out the side of your neck!" Felicia responded as she walked toward the door.

"Just ask your mother what she used to do for money to pay for her fancy degrees. How did she put herself through college, baby girl? She damn sure didn't have family here starting off. She's from the islands, right? I wonder how she came up so great. You've never questioned your mother's accomplishments, Felicia." Deangelo said as he tossed the change on the table to pay for the coffee.

Standing at the door Felicia stood in silence. She couldn't remember her mother working throughout her childhood. Felicia and her sister had never gone without anything. Everything was always paid for in cash whether it had been for school or clothes or a vehicle. Her mother never kept a paper trail to where her money came from, and the girls never had sense enough to question it or her.

"Felicia, listen please. I know this is a lot for you to process right now, but just make time to go see my brother please, before we all get killed," Deangelo replied.

Felicia turned and walked out the door taking everything Deangelo just said into consideration.

Arriving home she sat on the couch and replayed the conversation over in her head wondering what the big deal was about her mother and the jobs she used to do for people in her younger days.

Felicia's phone rang, startling her out of her thoughts. Caria was calling to apologize for missing several calls, but Felicia really didn't care to hear the details on what it was that Caria had gotten into.

"I was just hitting you up, lady, to see if you were still coming to get me?" Felicia asked.

"Felicia, you know I'll be over to get you, boo. Is everything okay?" Caria was concerned for Felicia because her tone was dry and she didn't seem to be enthused about the job or going in for training.

"I'm fine, Caria. I just have a lot on my mind, and I have no clue where to start when dealing with a load of bullshit."

"Well, Felicia, the best I can say right now is start where the main problem begins, love. Is this about last night?" Caria asked.

"*Nooo*," Felicia replied as she began to chuckle. "Last night was one of the most interesting experiences I've had in a while, not to mention very fun, or at least I thought we had fun. Didn't we?"

"Of course, I enjoyed every inch of you, boo. You're something special, and I really need you to know that, Felicia."

Felicia sat smiling from ear to ear forgetting about the problems in her life for just a moment.

"So are you going to tell me what's going on with you, babe?" Caria asked.

"Well, since we're on the subject, the guy whom I met in the club last night is the brother of the guy who raped me."

"*Felicia, what the fuck are you doing*? Why are you talking to him, or even entertaining the idea of those fools?" Caria shouted at Felicia.

"I know the shit sounds crazy, Caria, but it's some other shit going on; and honestly they have my attention right now. I can't just sit back and not do anything about it. I need to do this in order to get the answers I need."

"Felicia, what the fuck are you talking about? What fucking answers, and what do you have to do, babe?"

Felicia sat in silence on the phone daydreaming about childhood memories of people in and out of her life, the constant moving and paintings on the hotel walls until her mother finally settled down with Frank.

"*Felicia*, are you there?" Caria shouted through the phone bringing her back to reality.

"Yes, I'm here. Just think about how everything changed when my mother met Frank, Caria. It's some weird shit going on, and my parents are trying their best to keep me away from it, but the shit is finding me. Everything is unraveling in front of me!"

"I really think you should have a sit-down with your folks, babe, and talk to them before you go off and do something silly," Caria replied.

"So you think my finding out whom the fuck my parents are is silly, Caria?"

"No, boo, that's not what I meant. Listen. I understand you're upset, but please don't take it out on me or flip my words. I'm just asking: Do you think you should have a talk with them before you go off and do something you'll regret, love?"

"I understand what you're saying, Caria, and if I felt like what you were saying was some real shit, I would do it; but the fact that I'm twenty-six and I've never heard what my dad or mom has done for a living is a little unorthodox. They both attended top-notch colleges and graduated without any money having to be paid back; and then on top of that, I attended Yale, and everything was paid for—no bounced checks, nothing, Caria!" Felicia said sounding very irritated.

"I get it. There's no paper trail, but that still doesn't scream foul play to me, boo. It could have been government grants or some shit like that. They could have been in college from full scholarships or something, Felicia. However, I get it. This motherfucker pops up out of the blue with some bullshit and sweet-talks his way into your head. Who the fuck is this nigga?!"

"Old friend from my childhood after my folks settled down in the suburbs. They were the only other black people in the hood that I grew up in. My mom became a counselor when I was twelve, and my dad was a contractor for some company I couldn't tell you," Felicia replied.

"Well I obviously can't talk you out of something that's planted on your heart, boo. If you have to know, do your research, but going up there to that place alone is not bright at all."

Felicia became silent once more, while her friend ran down everything. She was up to. She knew exactly what it was that was going on, and it was a task she was willing to do if Felicia would have her but Felicia knew this was something that she had to do alone. As soon as Caria was done running down the plans of how everything could play out, Felicia responded changing the subject, "Now that you are on the phone with me and have everything figured out, tell me something, Caria. Where the hell did you go last night after you dropped me off because you hadn't been home? I called your house and that silly-ass cell phone of yours, and I just kept getting the voicemail."

Startled by Felicia's question, Caria sat in silence for a few seconds before she filled the speakers with laughter. "Girl, I had a detour, and let's leave it at that," Caria replied nervously.

"Basically, I wasn't enough. You had to go and get a late-night snack?" Felicia replied.

"Felicia, baby, let's get one thing understood right now. You're married, baby, and I'm not looking for anything serious. I like you a lot, but like I said you're married; and the fact that you're jealous is cute, but honestly, baby, what more could we possibly be, besides great friends with benefits?" Caria had just said a mouthful to Felicia, and although she understood the facts that Caria was stating, it still wasn't a pleasant feeling being told that you weren't enough.

"Well, Caria, I'll see you tonight," Felicia replied with a dry tone.

Caria could hear in Felicia's tone that she was hurt, but it was a must that she didn't forget that she was already in a relationship and Caria was not the one to play sideline forever. Hanging up the phone Caria was now upset with how everything just played out. She could have explained to Felicia that she already had somewhat of a relationship with Sage, but then that would open the doors up for more questions, and Caria was not ready. Sage was aware of Felicia, but Felicia had no clue as to whom Sage was. Caria had managed to keep her a secret, but now the thoughts had become haunting for her. If Felicia was flipping out over her parents not telling her what they did for a living, how the fuck would she react to her sleeping with a Wiccan?

The thought of losing Felicia as a friend devastated Caria. She had put in effort and time with this girl which was against her rules in the first place. Caria had never gotten attached to anyone, but here she was concerned about Felicia's feelings. It confused her to no end why was Felicia so important to her and why would she fall for someone with more issues than herself. Although Felicia's drama was minor in her eyes, Caria was still in the process of becoming a Wiccan herself. How would Felicia deal with that if they were to become steady in their relationship?

Caria wrecked her brain throughout the day thinking about Felicia and the crazy shit she was about to get herself into. *Why wouldn't she just face her parents and ask them what the hell they did for a living? And not only that, why does it fucking matter?* Caria thought out loud.

"At least she has parents to turn to when she needs them," Caria said while picking up the phone dialing out.

"Hello," a soft voice answered.

"How are you feeling, Ma?" Caria asked.

"I was fine, boo. I didn't think I would be hearing from you so soon, but now that I have, I'm feeling great," Sage replied filling the phone with laughter.

"Bitch, you know something is really wrong with you, right?" Caria replied, and they both chuckled.

"What's up, boo? What could I possible do for you?"

"Sage, I need to know how long it takes to become a full-fledge Wiccan."

"Why do you ask, Caria?"

"That's not how this works, Sage. I ask the questions. Then you give me answers, and then you can ask a question. Come on now. You know this, woman!" Caria chuckled.

"I understand that entirely, missy. I'm just curious as to why you want to know!"

"It's my business, Sage. Damn," Caria replied.

"Unfortunately, lady, when involved in what we're involved in, it's not just your business, baby girl. It's all our business to know what you're up to and whom you're about to practice certain spells on, Caria."

Caria sat in silence shocked that Sage was already aware as to what she had planned. "Sage, have you been watching me or something?" Caria asked.

"No, but I do know things, baby. My talents do work. You know that though," Sage replied sarcastically.

"Look, Sage. I'm not up to anything. I'm just eager to know and learn things that I've been promised and haven't been shown yet, but it's nothing. I'll move at your pace if that's what you want, Sage."

"Caria, I'm not as slow as you try to play me, baby girl. You're concerned for that little bitch. I'm not stupid, Caria, and the fact that you keep trying to play me like I am is really starting to piss me off. I should warn you to tread softly when fucking with me, little girl!"

"Sage, what the fuck are you talking about? Didn't we just spend an incredible night together? I'm pretty sure we did because I remember being there sucking on that little pussy, so please tell me what the fuck does Felicia have to do with what we got going on, boo?" Caria replied trying to throw Sage off.

"I'm not stupid, Caria. I knew when you did her reading without her that you had feelings for her. Just because you can't admit it to yourself doesn't mean people can't see what the fuck is going on. I just prefer for you not to lie to me about it. We are supposed to be upfront and honest with each other if this is ever going to work. I knew you and that girl were going to hook up. I've seen parts of it, and I was going to keep it to myself; but since you and *ol' girl* seem to be getting close, it's a must you know that darkness is coming for you," Sage replied bluntly.

"*What the fuck*, Sage?!"

"I'm just being honest, Caria. I've seen this. It's not some jealous tantrum. You said when you pulled the fucking cards on that little bitch, *Death* came up. Well, sweetheart, keep hanging with your newfound friend, and Death will be paying you a visit shortly."

Unable to continue the conversation, Caria slammed the phone down in Sage's ear. "How dare that bitch come at me like that! Fuck her. I don't need that bitch to become anything. I got me like I've always had me." As Caria went on with her pep talk, she could feel that something in Sage's words was the truth. Caria remembered the conversation that she and Sage had about the Death card not always belonging to the person that it had been pulled on. Death could be for anyone who was in that person's life at the time. Caria tried to gather her thoughts. *What if Sage is right? What if she did see me die?* It was the question that was going to taunt Caria all day. How could she be in a shitty situation like this? Caria's feelings for Sage hadn't changed, but the L word was approaching fast between her and Felicia; and she knew Sage wouldn't be able to handle it if she tried to leave her alone fully.

As the bells rang throughout the prison, Felicia tried to remain calm about the whole situation.

The prisoners walked through the doors, and Felicia was now face-to-face with Derek after all this time.

"So what the fuck could you possibly tell me about my mother, Derek? That's the only reason I agreed to come and do this fucked-up shit you call a visit!"

Derek smiled as he saw Felicia was still bitter about their last encounter. "Baby, there is no need to be that way, okay? The pussy was good, always have been good, so chill," Derek teased. Felicia could feel her blood boiling. Who the fuck was he? This was not the Derek she used to affiliate herself with back in the day.

"Derek, you've changed, dude. Like really, what the fuck happened to you? You used to be the sweetest guy around, and now you're this sick sadistic rapist. I seriously don't get it!" Derek just smiled as Felicia finished expressing her personal issue with him.

"Are you done?" Derek replied.

"Yeah, I guess I am. What do you want, fool? Why am I here?"

"Your mom works for the mafia."

"What? Is this the bullshit I drove sixty fucking miles for? My mom doesn't know the first thing about being in a fucking mafia, let alone working with them. I knew this was a sick trick to get me up here. What's next? You go try to rape me in the prison now?" Felicia replied laughing as she stood up like she was about to head for the exit.

"Bitch, you really need to get the fuck over yourself because if anything happens to my brother because of what your mother really is, I'm coming for you, and I'm going to finish the job!" Derek replied not cracking a smile.

"Listen here, prison bitch. You can talk all the shit you want. Nothing about you scares me. I fuck bitches bigger and tougher than you," Felicia responded.

Derek was shocked to see this side of Felicia. Nothing about her looked tough, but she had heart. "Listen. I don't have all day to play who has the bigger cock. Sit the fuck down so I can school you, Felicia. This shit is real, and the guy who leads it is real, and he's locked the fuck up in here. He has connections, Felicia. This dude isn't a fucking joke," Derek replied as he scanned the sitting room to see if anyone was paying attention to them.

Felicia could see that Derek's whole demeanor changed once he spoke of the mafia king.

"So what if I do believe you, Derek? What the fuck am I supposed to do?"

"You have to convince Sandy to go see Diablo and his mother."

"Derek, who the hell is Diablo and his mother? My mom doesn't know any people by the name of Diablo!" Felicia replied.

"Felicia, once you mention that name to your mother, you really need to pay close attention to her facial expressions and the body language. The way her body responds will let you know everything you need to know whether she's lying or telling the truth."

A silent Felicia sat and replayed her childhood over and over in her head. How could her mother have been a part of something so reckless and dangerous and not mention a word of it to her family?

"Derek, why did you rape me?"

Like a deer in headlights, Derek sat quietly before he gained the courage to explain that the rape was staged. He had to finish the deal that he had made with Diablo for his brother to live. Felicia had a new genre of information to take in, but her brain was starting to overload.

"Derek, I have to go. I have to find my mother," Felicia responded confused about everything.

"Hey, one more thing, Felicia, you have to come back; but the next time you come, you won't be meeting with me," he said as he dropped his head.

"What the fuck are you talking about, Derek?!"

"When you come back, you'll need to have your mother because you will be having a private visit with Diablo, and please don't try to stand him up, Felicia. This motherfucker has connections everywhere. You don't know who works for whom. Hell for all I know, he could already have someone set up with you, and you don't even know it."

Felicia looked at Derek as he seemed sincere, but the fact that he raped her shot that down.

"Derek, don't act like you care about my well-being. You did what you did for your brother, just like you are still doing what you do, just to keep your brother safe," Felicia replied.

"Felicia, you can believe what you want, baby. I've always loved you, and I've always cared for you. We just had different paths, baby, and I was okay with that. I've always kept a close eye on you though to make sure that nigga was treating you right."

"Yeah, I'm sure. Maybe that was the reason you came close to killing me that night at the gym, huh? You cared that much about me."

"Felicia, if I wanted you dead, baby, we both know it would've happened. I stalled, and you know it. I didn't have to rape you. I could have just killed your ass when you were in the dance studio. You really need to start paying more attention to your surroundings. You're blind to the fact that there are some fucked-up people out here in this world," Derek replied.

Felicia chuckled at Derek and the statement he was making. "You were always intelligent, Derek. It's just sad you're wasting yourself in a place like this."

"I'm waiting my talents out because I love my brother and I care for the only family that I have left. If you valued anything about your family, you would do as I'm telling you so you can live to give birth to one of my children," Derek replied trying to ease the moment between them.

They both laughed at the joke Derek had just made, but Felicia knew Derek had a point. Heading home Felicia replayed their conversation over and over trying to put the pieces together, but there was still too much information missing, so she had no choice but to bring up everything to her mother.

Arriving at her mother's house, Felicia spotted her mother's car in the garage, so it was now or never to find out what the hell was going on. Felicia parked and hopped out the vehicle. Knocking at the door she waited for someone to answer as she contemplated an icebreaker to all the questions that she had. There was no way around it. Nothing flowed, so she figured she would just come straight out with it as soon as she opened the door.

"Hey, Felicia, baby. How are you doing?" Sandy asked.

"I'm fine, Mom. How have you been?"

"Oh, I can't complain, baby. You should have called and told me you were coming over. I could have had something cooking," Sandy replied.

"Naw, I just came to talk, Mom. It's a few things I wanted to talk to you about, if you don't mind having a discussion with me," Felicia responded as she paced through her mother's manor.

"Shoot, Felicia. What's on your mind, baby girl?"

"Mom, what was your source of income when you were in college?"

"Umm, I worked all types of jobs to get me by, love. Why do you ask?" Sandy replied as she looked at Felicia with a strange look in her eyes.

"I just figured I'd ask because you and dad have never really talked about your past, and I figured now was better than any other to find out how my parents became such a success. I mean you started out with nothing. Now look at you guys. Mom, you have your own business, and Dad is retired from some job through the government. It's just amazing, and I would like to know how you got so far with no help or family being in the States, Mom."

Sandy was no fool. She could smell a rat from miles away, but the fact that this was her daughter asking put Sandy in a position to either tell the truth or keep quiet about the treacherous life she used to live.

"Honey, I don't think now is the time to talk about this; and honestly, I don't feel my past should be any concern of yours. Just know that mommy did what she could to do right by you and your sister growing up. I've worked hard to give you girls the life I never had, baby girl."

"Mom, I understand all of that and the fact that it seems like you're trying to keep something from me. Frank's been around for years, Mom, but he's not my father. He's Heather's. Who's my real father, Mom? How come you never speak of him to me? Do I not have the right to know whom I come from, whom I'm a part of?" Felicia replied with tears streaming down her face.

"Felicia, baby, where is this coming from? It's been twenty-six years, and now you start asking questions about things you could care less about once upon a time. I must know, baby girl, where these questions are coming from before I answer anything!" Sandy was confused and irritated by Felicia and the questions she was asking. "Why the sudden interest in my past? What happened to spark this shit, Felicia?"

"It's now or never!"

"What?" Sandy replied.

"Mom, I went to De'Shjine prison."

Without mumbling a word, Sandy rose from her seat and walked toward Felicia. *Slap!*

"You fucking idiot! That's why you're asking these fucking questions, *Felicia*! Do you have any idea what you've done?!" Sandi shouted.

"Mom, how was I to know you led a secret fucking life with the mob or whatever the hell they are!"

"Right now, all I need to know is whom did you talk to and what the hell you've told them, Felicia."

"I had to go see Derek."

"Why does that name sound familiar?" Sandy replied.

"It's the guy who raped me at the gym, Mom."

"Felicia, why would you go to prison just to see a guy who raped you against your will?" Sandy asked.

"You know, Mom, I've asked you like four questions and you haven't even considered answering one of them for me; but here you are asking me all these questions that you want answers to, and I can't even get one answer!" Felicia shouted.

"Felicia, what the hell do you honestly want to know, baby, the fact that you may have blown my cover or that I've been in hiding for over twenty years because I took my share of money from some people whom I used to work for back in the day?!"

"What was your share, Mom?" Felicia waited patiently on her response.

Sandy paced the room in silence and then turned toward Felicia with a smirk and replied, "It was 2.5 million dollars, baby girl. Now that you know, princess, tell me what the fuck could you honestly do with this type of weight? You couldn't stomach the life that I used to live. You couldn't handle the sacrifices that I had to make, *the people whom I had to bury*!"

"By bury, do you mean…"

"*Yes, Felicia*! I was a professional businesswoman. I worked for the head man. He set up the hits and I would take them out the game for him. See, your mother was a beautiful woman with a killer shot. You can kill any man if you use the right assets," Sandy replied as she chuckled with tears falling.

Felicia sat in silence as Sandy went on explaining the lifestyle that she was into before she got pregnant.

"Mom, you've told me everything except what I really want to hear."

"What else could you possibly need to know, Felicia?" Sandy asked as she stared out the bay windows.

"Who is my father, Mom?"

"Baby, Frank is your father."

"No, he isn't, Mom. That's Heather's father! Look. I might as well tell you I have to go back to the prison because they have my information, and I'm pretty sure whomever it is you're hiding from already knows where you reside. The fact that they found me without even knowing who I was, Mom, tells me that he already knew of your whereabouts and just wanted to send you a message by hurting me; but Derek couldn't kill me because he loves me, Mom! I was raped and damn near killed because of you, *Mom*! The guy who's in prison, the one demanding that I come back to see him, is that my father?" Felicia asked.

"No, that's not your father, sweetie. He's your half-brother."

"*What*? So you're saying that I have an Italian brother?"

"Yes, his mother was the reason everything went sour in the first place, but it's a long story," Sandy replied.

"Mom, please all I have left is time."

Sandy continued to stare out the window with her mind blown that her daughter was finally asking questions about the past. She always knew the time would come, but nothing could ever prepare her for it. Her heart was heavy as she relived the past once more for her daughter's sake.

"Baby girl, your real father wants nothing to do with you, and we should just leave it at that."

"What do you mean he wants nothing to do with me, Mom? He doesn't even know me. Does he know that I even exist, Mom?"

"Yes, Felicia, he knows! He's the reason I took the money and ran. He wanted me to kill you, baby girl. He didn't want anything to do with a colored child," Sandy replied as she dropped to her knees in tears. The love that she thought she buried years ago came rushing back causing an overwhelming feeling.

"*Mom*, are you okay?!" Felicia shouted.

"I'm fine, baby girl. I might as well tell you I've said this much, huh?" Sandy chuckled. "Felicia, when I was seventeen, I came to the States for a better future. We had no family here, so once I landed here Troy was the first guy whom I ran into, lost in the streets of LA. Troy was a sight for sore eyes and every young girl's nightmare. I had no clue as to what I was getting myself into when I met that handsome devil. He showed me the ropes of the dope game. It started off small, and then it progressed. Troy had big goals for me. He always told me, 'Sandra, get to school. I need a lawyer to get me out when I get locked up.' I loved that man with my soul, baby. I always felt it was me and him against the world for years until one night he threw a party. That's when I met Saunte."

Felicia could tell by the growl in Sandy's tone that she didn't like this woman she spoke of. "What does she have to do with anything, Mom?"

"Like I said Troy and I were doing rather good with our business. Everything was building up; and as soon as he laid eyes on that gold-digging bitch, he called himself putting me on the back burner, after five fucking years of me being by his side all hours of the night packaging shit and counting money making sure everything evened out and then going to school during the day to get an education to help further myself for *us*! I was a virgin to life when I met your dad, and that man opened me up in every way that he could. He knew he had me around his finger and fiddle me whenever he wanted to. I would be anything for him. That's how in love I was with that man, until she came into the picture and took him from me. What I always thought was crazy. Although he was with her, he would still come sleep in my bed at night. It was confusing for me because I loved him so much and he took it for granted. I honestly wish I had figured that out then, but by the time I came to my senses, I was already five months' pregnant and Saunte was due. It broke my heart when I found out they were sharing the same moments that he and I were sharing. Saunte got to live her pregnancy in the open, while I had to be hidden. After she gave birth to his precious baby boy, Troy felt his mission for a kid was over. I woke up to him in my apartment one night sitting on the edge of my bed. I'll never forget the look in his eyes or the evil in his voice when he said the bullshit that he said to me." Sandy couldn't bring herself to repeat his words. She placed both hands over her face and began to sob more.

Felicia could see that reliving the past was hard for her mother, but she needed to know everything if she was going to figure out a plan to resolve the shit that was going on.

"Mom, I'm sorry, but I really need to know what all happened, all the way up to you getting away from them."

"Felicia, as your dad sat on the bed, he told me to get rid of you. He had his bundle of joy, and it was by the woman he was meant to be with. I didn't understand why he would sleep with me if he was so in love with that woman. Even before I got pregnant, I would try to see other guys, but he'd show up to the place and beat the crap out of me and the guys would always go missing. He didn't want me in Saunte's presence, but he would punish me if I showed another man my affection. He pulled out his pistol the night I refused to get rid of you, and he beat me with it. He told me to get the abortion, or he would do it for me. I knew then what I felt for him wasn't genuine. How could he beat the woman he claimed he loved with a pistol? Fifty-seven stitches and a baby's heart barely beating was an eye-opener for me. I planned to stick it to him and that bitch Saunte. She filled Troy's head with malicious, ideas about me. She told him I was sleeping with the help and that's whom the baby belonged to. In my heart Troy knew you belong to him, but he chose her and his son over us after everything I helped build. They lived like gods, and she tore everything down that I worked my ass off for. My heart and soul, I put into that man, baby girl. I took out all of his competition. I even made a little name in the streets. They called me the Sexy Sandy."

"Mom, how did you escape him?" Felicia replied.

"Well, since I was over everything, I just went to the banks and started clearing out all the accounts that my name was on. I figured I would hit that first. Then afterward I went back to the house he bought, and I packed my most valuable assets and then drove by their house to drop off my latest gift which was a homemade bomb I had been working on. It was my very first one, and I must admit I was quite proud when I heard that Saunte was the one who found it, but it affected Troy in a different way when he noticed his love was missing half her face and an arm."

Sandy shook her head and chuckled.

"*Mom, you could have killed her*!" Felicia shouted.

"What the hell do you want from me, Felicia?! I was a *kid who was pregnant for the first time, in love with a man whom my world revolved around*! He broke my heart, so you tell me: What was I supposed to do? He trained me to be a heartless killer, not a heartless lover. At nineteen he had me shoot a guy in the head for disrespecting us. It was my first kill and the first time he decided to take my virginity from me. He taught me everything, and he taught me well." Sandy stood in hopes that Felicia would be over this whole meeting her father.

Felicia understood the consequences, but it was a whole new list of shit that she had just been hit with as she followed Sandy out of the room.

"Mom, what happens now?"

"What do you mean, baby girl?"

"Well, I'm supposed to go back to the prison to meet Diablo, and he wants you to come with me, Mom."

"I tell you what, Felicia. Since you're so into doing the right thing, you can go without me, but I'm warning you now. Those people are not what you're ready for. You'll do good if you just stay away from them. We can move because I have money, baby girl. We don't have to stay here."

"Mom. Do you always run? I mean you're a hit woman. Why are you always running?"

"Because, baby, they have way more firepower than I have and this is personal. It's not just business. I'll fight if I have to; however, we don't have to. We have money to just uproot and go somewhere else to rebuild."

Felicia was hearing everything her mother was saying, but she wasn't feeling it. Hugging her mother she grabbed her keys and headed out the house to her vehicle. Felicia thought about everything her mother had just told her and added the parts from Derek. The problem was Troy and Diablo. She thought if she could get through to Diablo, maybe things could be settled. She picked up her phone to call Ron.

It had been almost a week since she last saw him, and she was still concerned about his well-being, and the fact he hadn't been by the house to see the boys was really starting to bug her out. It wasn't like Ron to just disappear nor miss any time with his Boys. The phone rang and rang until the voicemail picked up. Felicia left a message informing him of newfound information that just struck her life as she pulled out of her mother's driveway. After leaving her message with Ron, Felicia called Caria. The time was getting close for the girls to meet up to plan the fittings for the club promotion tonight. Although Felicia had a lot on her plate, she decided to try and hide her emotions the best she could.

"Hello, love, what's up?" Caria answered.

"Hey, boo, do you think I could roll with you kind of early today?"

"Sure, are you home?"

"No, but I will be in about twenty minutes if you could just wait on me? I promise it won't take me long," Felicia replied.

"Sure, I'll meet you there in twenty."

Arriving at the house Caria waited for Felicia, as she too had some information to share with her. As she waited Ron pulled up behind her in the driveway.

"Oh great, this asshole," Caria said to herself as Ron stood outside of his car with the facial expression as to why she was sitting in his driveway and Felicia wasn't home.

"You want to get this piece of shit out of my driveway so I can park my fucking car?" Ron shouted. Caria sat in her vehicle like she hadn't heard a word that came out of Ron's mouth. Ron walked over to her and hit her window with his fist. "Get the fuck out of my driveway so I can park my fucking car please!"

Caria stepped out of her vehicle with a gun in her hand, so Ron could see that she was not playing with him, but Ron called her bluff anyway.

"Bitch, you're in front of my house waiting for my wife with your nasty ass and you pull a gun out on me?! You knew she was married before you placed those demon hands on her," Ron said in a stern voice.

Caria couldn't do anything except laugh. "You think I stole your bitch? Is that the reason you're upset?" She continued to laugh.

"Keep laughing, bitch, and I'll knock your fucking teeth down your throat," Ron replied to her chuckles.

Caria saw that Ron was upset and was smelling the liquor on his breath as he voiced his opinions to her. Caria knew Ron wasn't playing, so she chose to say her next words. She cocked her pistol along with them. "Listen, Ron. I never intended for any of this to happen—" Caria tried to explain but got interrupted.

"Before you start your fucking lying, all I'm going to mention is that fucking party where you two were grinding on each other like I wasn't there. Like I said you knew she was married, and you didn't give one fuck about it! But I guess I should have expected that from some low-class lesbian *bitch*!"

Caria stood there in silence for a few moments before she replied. "Ron, I didn't take shit that didn't want to be taken in the first place. You're mad at me because you can't satisfy your wife. That is not my fault nor my problem, and FYI she came on to me. She confessed to me that she wanted to eat my pussy. It wasn't the other way around. Although she tasted just as sweet as me, I didn't volunteer my services; she wanted my services. From what I was told, you could use some of my techniques on eating pussy," Caria replied to his disrespectful comment.

Ron balled his fist and punched through her back window and began to walk closer to her with his eyes glaring.

"Ron, if you touch me, I'm going to shoot your ass; and I'm not playing with you, drunk or not!" Caria shouted. As Felicia pulled up she could see there was a problem. Broken glass was on the ground, and Caria was standing outside of her car with a gun pointed at her husband.

"What the hell are you two doing?" Felicia shouted from her car still trying to place it in park as she hopped out.

"So you seriously slept with this bitch, Felicia?" Ron shouted as tears flowed down his face.

"Ron, please let me explain!"

"Naw, we're good, Felicia. That was the last straw. I'm done!" Ron yelled as he walked off throwing his hands in the air.

"*Ron, please*! Wait. Let me explain. Please, Ron!" Felicia shouted as she started to cry.

Ron continued to walk away. His heart couldn't take it any longer. He got into his vehicle and sped out the yard and into the street with his tires screeching down the road. Felicia fell to her knees in tears. Her heart had just decided as it was breaking that she was still very much in love with her husband, but it was now too late to say anything or do anything about it. Felicia turned to Caria with teary red eyes.

"What did you say to him, Caria?"

"*What*?! So you're going to pin this shit on me? He's the one who came for me. As you can see he broke my fucking car window, Felicia!"

"But what did you say to make him react like this? He's never been this upset! *What* the fuck did you say to him, Caria?!" Felicia cried out.

"What do you want to hear, Felicia? That I told him the truth about us being attracted to one another or the part where we've been spending a lot of time with each other? Or about the part where we fucked each other's brains out? Or how about the part where you eat pussy like a fucking champ?! Is that what the fuck you want to hear, Felicia? Somebody got to tell the fucking truth. It might as well be me since you two were so fucked up you couldn't communicate right."

"You fucking bitch!" Felicia responded still sobbing.

"I guess I'll be the bad guy in your fucked-up world, but remember this, bitch: I didn't do anything that you didn't want, so make sure you tell yourself that in between the lies," Caria replied.

"Get the fuck away from my house. I can't stand to look at you, bitch!"

"Fine with me. Get the fuck out of the way so I can go! As for tonight find your own fucking way to the club, bitch, and don't expect for me to help you with shit!" Caria replied getting into her car speeding off.

Felicia went into the house and called Ron hoping he would pick up, but it went straight to voicemail. She never got the chance to discuss with Ron or Caria the prison situation or the information that her mother had just shared with her. Felicia's world was crashing down around her, and there was nothing she could do to stop it. How would she go to work tonight with her and Caria becoming enemies? How would she make it through this war that was approaching her fast without her husband by her side to provide his strength? Felicia was left heartbroken, but she knew she couldn't focus on that for long. She had business to handle because if she ignored the problem, she would be the one to end up dead.

Felicia returned to the prison on Friday like she was asked to in spite of everything that was going wrong in her life. A part of Felicia was nervous, but the other half was very curious as to whom this Diablo guy was. Although Sandy explained the past, Felicia still felt a void in her heart.

If her mother could keep her past a secret for all these years, she wondered what else her mother was hiding as she sat there waiting for the prisoners to be released for visitation. The bells rang throughout the prison, and Felicia's heart began to thump faster and harder as she watched every prisoner come through the doors. She wondered to herself what this guy's attitude was going to be like. Would he be excited to see her, or did he have any idea that she was his sister from another woman? Then reality sat in as she thought, *What if he tries to harm me just to get back at my mother?* She decided to do something crazy like shake the thoughts out of her mind and give him a chance before she bolted out of there.

"So you're Felicia?"

Chills ran through her body as she came to a stand and slowly turned in the direction of the voice behind her. She locked eyes with a pure Italian with silky black hair and big brown eyes with a smile that could awake the gods.

"*Umm*, yes, I'm Felicia. And you're Diablo," Felicia replied.

"I am." He smirked at her. "Please take a seat," he said as he sat down.

Felicia couldn't get over how attractive this guy was, and she was related to this guy.

Felicia smiled at him. "So what can I do for you? I've already heard both sides of the story from my mom and the message you sent through Derek, which I might add was very foul."

Diablo didn't utter a word. He just sat there taking in her beautiful smile and her smooth skin.

"You know you are way more beautiful in person. I had no idea I had a baby sister this damn fine. I kind of feel like an asshole with the whole rape thing." He chuckled in her face.

"If you don't mind my asking, why would you want to harm a complete stranger? I mean you don't even know me. You don't know if I have children or anything. You're just willing to take lives for no reason?" Felicia asked.

"Well, I highly doubt that you have children especially since I know everything there is to know about you, Felicia. I know your mother, and I know she's married to an ex-FBI agent who still works for the government secretly. I know way more than you put off, Ms. Felicia."

Felicia sat in silence with a strange look on her face as Diablo continued to tell her things that she had no clue of.

"Wait. So you're telling me that my step dad works for the government?" Felicia responded to the accusations that were being stated.

"Don't play innocent with me, girl. I know you know more than what you're putting off."

"Diablo, I'm not sure what you're looking for or what information you plan to gather from me, but I just found out less than twenty-four hours ago what my mom did for a living back in the day; and as for my step father, I had no clue what he did until now. I planned on gathering information on our real father, Diablo. That's the only reason I'm here. I want to know why he wanted you to live and me to die."

"I'm not here to play the fucking family, man. I want my fucking money that your mother stole from my family years ago! The only reason we haven't come for her is because of my father! After your whore of a mother disappeared, things got rough for my family. I mean after all it was your mother who planted that fucking bomb on my mom's porch to kill her," Diablo replied.

"Diablo, that has nothing to do with me, but the fact that my mother went through great lengths to get to your mother means that she was really in love with the asshole you call your father! The fact that he made her like that after they got their little business started was utterly fucked up. The fact that you find nothing wrong with it is fucked up. I say your mother got what the fuck she deserved!" Felicia replied.

As Felicia spoke freely, her words echoed throughout the visiting room bringing silence and attention toward her and Diablo. The words stung Diablo like salt being poured on an open wound. Before Felicia knew it Diablo reached across the table and had her in the air choked up.

"Get one thing straight, bitch. My mother didn't deserve any of that bullshit that happened; and for that statement, bitch, I claim your life!"

Guards shouting through the visiting room was the last thing Felicia heard before she was unconscious. Felicia woke to Deangelo wiping her face with a cold cloth.

"Welcome back, lady!"

Felicia smiled. "Well, that wasn't so bad. I thought he actually claimed my life." She chuckled.

"Felicia, this is getting dangerous. If I hadn't made it to you in time, he would have killed you. You need to convince your mother to give him what he wants and fast, Felicia!" Deangelo responded.

"I honestly don't think he's after money. I believe he wants me and my mother dead. I'm just not sure as to why. He couldn't possibly think that my mother still has that money that she took from them years ago, and not only that, but that money that he's bitching about was money owed to her for pain and suffering. So fuck him," Felicia replied to Deangelo.

"Felicia, I honestly think you and your mother should leave the States because something tells me shit just hit the fan. I'm not sure what your conversation was about, but he was really gunning to kill you, so the game stops here. I'm getting Derek transferred to another prison, and he's going to be placed in solitary for his safety, and as for myself, I'm leaving the States!" Deangelo responded.

"So that's it, D? You're just going to run?"

"Yes, Felicia. What would you have me do? Stay here and die?! You still think this is a game after witnessing firsthand that this dude doesn't give two shits about us or you! He can care less that you're his sister. Hell, as far as we know, that could be a lie. We don't know!"

"We do fucking know. My mother wouldn't lie about shit like that, and I'm not running. I'm staying, and I'm going to get to the bottom of this," Felicia replied.

Felicia came to a stand and walked toward the exit doors of the prison. Leaving out she noticed a vehicle that resembled Caria's. She thought to herself what the hell would Caria be doing here and whom she would have been seeing, but then she flushed the thoughts out of her head. Caria's driver side window was busted due to Ron and his temper tantrum, so there was no way she could have gotten it fixed that fast. She continued to walk past the vehicle to hers.

After a few days alone with her thoughts, she figured it would be best if she just continued to work for the airport especially since things went sour between Caria and her. Thinking about the situation that caused their falling out, she decided to call Ron to see if she could resolve the problem that occurred, but every time she called she got the voicemail.

"Where the hell is he, and what could he be doing, the reason he was ignoring me so tough?" she questioned. Then her phone rang back. "Hello, Ron," she answered.

"Aaw, baby sister, I hope you said goodbye to your friend," Diablo said as he chuckled through the speaker.

"What the fuck do you want, Diablo? You don't scare me like you think you do!"

"I'm glad you stated that because I'll be seeing you soon, bitch. *You're next*!" *Click!*

Felicia sat on the other end of the line listening to the dial tone as her heart dropped. Ron wasn't answering his phone, and then Diablo's words struck a blow. "Did I say goodbye?" The phone rang again. "What the fuck did you do, Diablo?"

"Felicia, it's me, Deangelo. That motherfucker killed Derek last night."

"*What*?!"

"He waited until everybody was down, and somehow they got into Derek's cell and beat him so bad he had to go to the infirmary, and that's where one of the inmates shanked him to death. I told you that motherfucker wasn't playing, bitch; but you just had to push, didn't you?! He was my only fucking family left, and now he's gone because of you, *bitch*!" Deangelo yelled through the phone still sobbing.

"D, baby, that's not my fault. Derek was a big boy!" *Click!* Felicia sat at the end of another conversation with the dial tone. "Hello. Hello!" Felicia shouted. With her heart lifted just a bit, she was relieved that it was Derek and not Ron. Derek was dead, and Diablo was on his way for her with Deangelo not too far behind. Shit was getting real really fast, and she knew she couldn't handle this alone. She needed help, but everybody in her circle was now pissed at her.

Desperate and scared Felicia went to the club in hopes that she would find Caria because Ron still wasn't taking her calls and shit was becoming clear that this was not a game. Caria was working at the bar when she looked up and saw Felicia walking toward her.

"To what do I owe the pleasure? Did Ron finally divorce your ass?" Caria said with a smirk.

Felicia didn't find the joke funny at all. She was scared for her life, and she needed help. She stared at Caria with tears streaming down her face. The one person who could keep her mind steady and make her feel at ease was missing, and she was more than worried.

"I can't find Ron, and the guy from the prison killed Derek to send me a message that he wasn't playing games anymore. Now D is looking for me, and I have no one to turn to or talk to, Caria." She broke down in Caria's face stirring something in her.

"Emotions, oh my god, I don't fucking cry, Felicia. What the hell have you done to me?" Caria poked jokes as they both chuckled still crying.

"Could you take a break, so we can talk please?"

"Yeah, just give me a minute. I'll meet you around the corner by the restrooms," Caria replied.

Felicia walked off, and Caria dried her eyes as she pulled her phone out and dialed Sage.

"Hey, baby, I need to see you tonight and I'm bringing someone with me; and before you ask, yes, it's Felicia. Her husband has gone missing, and we really need to find him. Something tells me he's not doing so good wherever the hell he is."

"Bring her over after midnight," Sage replied.

"But, Sage, that's like three hours away. What the hell are we going to do until midnight?" Caria asked.

"Sounds like a personal problem, sweetie. I have business jumping off right now, and I'll be free to do stuff for free around midnight. Take it or leave it, love."

"*Fine*," Caria replied. "I'll see you around midnight." Caria hung up the phone and walked around the corner to Felicia with a bottle of Crown Royal and two shot glasses. "Here, take these to the head, and then we can talk afterward."

Felicia smiled as her tears were still streaming. Her feelings conflicted because she was happy she and Caria were with each other but sad because she wanted Ron by her side. She wanted him home and safe. She tossed the first shot back.

"Felicia, let me apologize for the way I acted at your house, boo. I had no right to disrespect your husband, although he started it, but that's not the point." Caria chuckled as she went on apologizing. "I had no right telling your husband about us, and for that I apologize."

Felicia smiled at Caria and replied, "I accept your apology, boo, but I honestly just wanted you to help me find Ron. I really miss him, Caria, and I love him; and I do want to make it work with my husband. I too want to apologize for what I've put you through and the position I've placed you in. I had no right putting you in harm's way. I let things get too far out of hand although I enjoyed every bit of what you offered me. I just really want to find Ron so I can tell him that I'm sorry and that he is enough for me. He's everything a woman could ever ask for, Caria, and I was lucky enough to get his heart." Felicia's heart broke thinking what if she never got the chance to tell him that.

"Don't talk like that, Felicia. You sound like he's already gone or you're about to go. What the hell is going on?"

Before Felicia could explain the TV flashed, catching Felicia's eye where she saw Diablo's face on the big screen. There was a prison break. Diablo and several others had managed to escape. Felicia focused on the TV trying to see if they could give a location or area he could be in, while Caria continued to talk.

"*Caria, that's him*!" Felicia jumped out of her seat.

"Who is *him*?"

"That's the Diablo guy who's coming for me and my mother. He's trying to kill us if we don't kill him first!" Felicia shouted.

"Wait. Explain to me what's going on, and don't leave anything out, *Felicia*!"

"I went to the prison the first time to see Derek, and he explained all this shit about my mother; and once I spoke to my mother, she explained that the shit Derek said was true. I also found out that Diablo, the guy you just saw on TV, is my half-brother by this mafia bitch, not to mention my mother was a professional hit woman—"

Caria interrupted. "So let me get this straight. You went to the prison to see the guy who raped you, after I told you not to, just to find out that your mother was a paid murderer which she confessed. Am I up to speed?" Caria asked with a jolted look on her face.

"You're coming, but you're not quite there. My mother doesn't want to go after these bastards for some reason, and that's what makes me nervous because I've never seen my mother run from anything, but for some reason she spooked. So that made me curious as to whom the fuck these people were because my mom didn't scare so easily. I went back to the prison to meet Diablo just like Derek asked me to, and that's when I found out about my step dad, who turned out to be government material; but neither of my parents want to confront these assholes. They'd rather pack up and leave for the islands, and I'm not feeling it, Caria!"

Caria sat in silence taking in everything that Felicia had dropped on her.

"Derek was murdered last night, Caria, and Deangelo is looking for me. He's trying to pin Derek's death on me, saying it's my fault that his brother is dead. Caria, I don't know what to do. I mean I'm my mother's child, but I can't kill anyone, but I don't want to run either. I love it here and the life I've helped my husband build. I'm not ready to give it up." She began to cry again.

"Hey, ladies, what are you doing in here? The club is about to open for business in twenty minutes. I need you dressed for the opening event, Felicia."

Felicia lifted her head after hearing her name from a familiar voice. "Derrell?"

"It's Mr. Werth. I'm only Derrell when I'm in costume." He smiled at her.

"Umm, sir, I'm having—"

"I understand you're having personal issues. I can see the tears, but I need workers tonight, not babies. You have the sources to save you, but it's up to you on what you're willing to do for the help, ladies." He smiled at the both of them again and walked out of the VIP section.

"Caria, what the fuck is he talking about?"

Caria smiled before she answered Felicia's question. "I guess he's willing to help us with our problem. Like he said, you have all the sources that you need. You just have to figure out what you're willing to do to get his help. I'm going to assume it has something to do with upstairs. If you haven't noticed, Mr. Werth is a bit of a freak, but I trust him; and besides we need his help finding Ron before your psycho brother finds you! How long has he been out?"

"I'm not sure, Caria. I just found out about the escape right here with you."

"*Shit*," Caria replied. "Well, the most we can do is keep you safe tonight. What other place would be safer than this place here? I mean your brother doesn't seem like the type of guy who would hang around a place like this."

"Yeah, but Deangelo knows exactly where to find me if he's coming for me."

"I still say you're safer here. After all you and Mr. Werth are on a first-name basis, so I'm sure he got some weight to keep us safe. Just get dressed, and I have something for you to put in your costume that will give you some peace of mind, okay? Tonight there's some rapper in town, and they're having their after-party here. So stick close to me behind the bar, and after we're done entertaining we can talk to Derrell on finding Ron, and then we can go from there to my girl's house so she can read the cards to see if he's safe."

Felicia glared at Caria when she heard her utter the words "girl's house." Caria saw that it struck a nerve, but it wasn't the time to play jealous. They had to move fast on their plan because death was approaching. Felicia got dressed to help out the bar when she passed a mirror and got a glimpse of herself. She didn't recognize the woman staring back at her. She had become dark with her makeup and her hair. Who was this woman in these skimpy clothes and hooker heels?

"Maybe I was born into death for a reason." She shook her head.

"*Come on!*" Caria yelled through the curtains.

Three hours into the night, Felicia couldn't help but wonder what if Diablo had gotten to Ron and he was now dead. Could that be the reason he wasn't answering his phone? Caria saw that Felicia was strapped in her thoughts again. She had to figure out how to get her attention to bring her back to reality. Before Caria could say anything, Derrell appeared at the bar.

"*Hey*! I'm not paying you to dwell on shit. I'm paying you to serve the drinks, *baby girl*!"

Snapping back, Felicia smiled with watery eyes. "My apologies, sir. I'm back and ready to stay focused," she responded as she continued to fight the tears away with her crooked smile.

"Meet me in my office after closing time and make sure that Caria comes. I have a proposition for you two ladies, and please stop crying. I'm sure your husband is fine and doing well. Men need time to get over bullshit whatever the bullshit is that you've done. Just know he's okay and he'll contact you when he's ready, okay?" Derrell said.

The words were comforting for Felicia as Derrell walked away from her and continued the night out. She served drinks and pushed the drama in her life far to the back of her head. The more she drank with the customers, the more her night seemed to feel lighter. Closing hours approached fast as they got the last straggling customer out the club. The girls headed up to Derrell's office sharing assumptions on what he might want and how far was he willing to go to help them since it was a mafia king coming to claim Felicia's life. Entering the office the girls were nervous. The scent of leather and citrus filled their noses. Derrell sat at his desk shirtless with a whip across his desk.

"Felicia, state your case," Derrell said.

Staring at Caria, Felicia began to explain what it was she was going through from the top to the bottom. As Felicia talked about her situation, Derrell was undressing both girls with his eyes. He couldn't shake the images of the girls together out of his head. The more she talked, the more he thought about it, and his dick began to harden as his breathing became heavier. Caria could tell something was going on with him as Felicia talked on not realizing anything.

"Excuse me, Mr. Werth, but to make a long story short, there's an escaped convict after her and trying to kill her. Bottom line, we have to get to this fucker before he gets us. Will you be able to help or not? We don't have time to sit around and wait for him to come for *us*!" Caria shouted.

"Well, being in my line of work, patience is everything, young Caria. The more you learn about your enemy, the better approach you can take. Felicia, that's exactly what you need to do. Wait for him to come to you! After all who knows you better than you? You can't go on his turf looking for him and expect to win, ladies. You get him on your turf, and that's how you'll beat him," Derrell replied.

"But he has guns and shit. How do I fight when he's not fighting fair?" Felicia replied.

"Who said anything about fighting fair, baby girl? Follow me." He stood up from his desk and headed out the office. Derrell took the girls down to the basement of the club. "What I'm about to show you needs to stay among us three. If you blab my business to anyone, the convict will be the last person you two need to worry about." Derrell opened the door, and guns were hanging everywhere as they walked in the room looking at all the weapons from wall to wall. Derrell schooled them on each weapon that they picked up.

With an unsettling feeling Felicia turned and looked at Derrell and remembered the words from Derek. Diablo could have anybody working for him. "Derrell, you're not just a club owner, are you?" Felicia asked looking at Derrell.

Derrell smiled and then replied, "I'm a man of many things, Ms. Felicia. The fact that I've shown you this room is letting you know I'm willing to help you, right?"

"Yeah, I understand you're willing to help, but please forgive me if I don't dive nose-deep into whatever the fuck you're serving!" Felicia snapped.

Derrell filled the gun room with laughter as Caria stood looking at both of them clueless to what had just happened. "What reason would I have to harm you, Felicia?"

"What reason would you have to be helping me, Derrell?"

"Let's just say that your kin to some very close friends of mine, and I will not elaborate on anything else. All I need to know is: Do you want my help or not?"

Felicia and Caria looked at each other and then back at him as they nodded their heads yes, out of options and nowhere else to turn.

"What do you want from us, Mr. Werth?" Caria asked.

"He wants what he hasn't had yet. Am I right?" Felicia replied.

Derrell smiled. "We have important matters to discuss, Ms. Felicia." He smirked and placed his shotgun back on the shelf.

Felicia and Caria went back and forth with Derrell for the plan to stop Diablo when Felicia's phone rang. Looking at the incoming call, she saw it was Heather whom she hadn't spoken to for quite some time, but now wasn't the time to be taking calls. She ignored the call to finish her conversation with Caria. Then it rang again.

"Gosh, Heather, what is it?"

"Now that's no way for you to talk to baby sis," a male voice replied.

"*Who is this?!*"

Chuckles filled the speaker.

"*Who the fuck is this?! Where is my sister?! If you fucking touch her, I'll slit your fucking throat.*" Tears flowed from Felicia's eyes.

"Oh, don't worry, baby girl. Our baby sister is fine. I haven't done anything to her yet." He laughed again.

"Diablo—"

"Shut the fuck up!" he interrupted. "You're not running shit, so stop acting like you are. It's time we talk business. If my standards are met, your sister can walk; but if you try anything stupid, you'll be fishing for her body parts all over the west coast. Am I understood?"

Quiet on the other line, Felicia trembled from his cold tone. "I understand, Diablo. Just please don't hurt my sister," Felicia pleaded.

"Where is your mother, Felicia?"

"I don't know. She disappeared right after our conversation a few days ago, Diablo. I haven't seen her since," Felicia replied.

"You got twenty-four hours to find her. For every hour after your time is up, just think about your sister and the torment she'll be facing. And baby girl?"

"What?"

"I need you to put yourself in your sister's shoes. She's with six of us, and we haven't been around anything this young and fresh. She's *beautiful*, Felicia."

"*Don't you fucking touch her*!"

"Have you ever had it rough, baby sis?" Diablo teased at Felicia. "Have you ever had that tight little asshole played with little momma?" He chuckled in Felicia's ear once more. Then *click!*

"*Hello! Hello! No, no, no! What the fuck!*" Felicia shouted as her legs became noodles falling to her knees crying hysterically.

"Felicia, baby, get up and try to get a hold of yourself. He's trying to fuck with your head. Don't let him. We got to stay focused. Now think. Can you think of any way to get in touch with your mother?" Caria asked.

"We have to figure out where the call was coming from," Derrell said.

"I don't know where she is. She stopped answering her phone, like I said, after that conversation I had with her!" Felicia broke down again.

"Caria, try calling from your phone," Derrell said.

Both phones went straight to voicemail. "*Shit*!" Caria replied.

"What happened?" Felicia asked when her phone rang again. "Hello, Heather," Felicia answered.

"No, it's me, Ron."

"Thank God you're okay, Ron. I've been calling you, baby! They have my sister."

"*Who*?" There was silence. "*Who has Heather, Felicia*?" Ron asked with anger in his voice.

"I have a half-brother whom my mother neglected to tell me about who's trying to kill me because my mom stole money from his family back in the day. He escaped from prison after killing Derek, and now he has Heather, and I can't locate my parents! And that's everything in a nutshell," Felicia replied.

"Where are you, Felicia?"

She sighed. "I'm with Caria, and before you go there, she's been the only one helping me through this bullshit when everyone else disappeared, baby."

"Felicia, what's the address to the club?" Ron asked.

Meanwhile Derrell was having a hard time locating the signal from Heather's phone. Felicia gave the address as she turned to Caria for comfort. First, her mother was missing, and now Heather was becoming overbearing.

"I really just need you two to get along. Try to work together for the sake of my family," Felicia muffled words into Caria's shoulder as she hugged her tight.

"Felicia, baby, you have nothing to worry about. Ron and I are going to be *best fucking friends*!"

Felicia smirked. "I need my sister. I can't let anything happen to her. She's my world." Felicia sobbed.

"Nothing is going to happen to Heather, baby. We'll get her back. I'm on my way to the club, so I'll see you in a few!" They hung up the phone.

"Come with me, Felicia," Derrell said.

Felicia followed him into a dark room. "Where are we going?" she asked.

"You're going to lie down for a few hours, love."

"No, I have to help with finding my people, *Derrell*!" she shouted.

"Look. He gave you twenty-four hours which is a nice amount of time for me to do my thing! I need you to be clearheaded, not foggy and stressed from no sleep and overthinking, love. Let me do my thing while you get some rest. Caria will be close by, and as soon as your husband gets here, I'll send him back."

Derrell walked over to the bar and put together two cocktails for himself and Felicia. As soon as the drink was in Felicia's hand, it was chugged and over. She handed the glass back to him and lay across the bed. Derrell headed toward the door flipping the light switch and closing the door behind him.

"How is she?"

"She'll be fine. She just needs to get some rest."

"Derrell, you should know that (sigh) Ron and I don't really get along all that well nor do I trust him, so this is about to be very interesting working with this maniac." Derrell laughed at the comment that was just made. "What's so funny?" Caria asked.

"Well, you are!"

"Elaborate please!"

"Let's see. You moved in on a married woman, and not only did you succeed in fucking her, but you made her fall in love with you knowing she was in a very vulnerable state in her life. However, the hilarious part is you fell in love with the married woman. Damn, baby."

"What the hell are you talking about, Derrell?"

"You can play the denial thing with me, or you can just go ahead and keep it real with me because I'm trained to detect when someone is lying to me, so it's your turn. Tell me I'm wrong." He walked toward her looking deep into her eyes.

"I have no reason to lie about anything. Everything you said is correct, but trying to get her husband to understand is a whole other story," Caria replied.

"Could you blame him for being pissed? You took the only thing he's probably ever loved in life away from him!"

"I didn't take shit. *She chose to come to me*! But she also wants to be with her husband. I have no problem with men. They just tend to not like me as much because I'm too independent for them."

"*Bullshit*! Caria, you don't want a man because you're afraid of submitting to us *men* which tells me one of two things has happened to you: Either you've been molested as a child or you were involved with an abusive asshole and that's what made you change your roles. You gave up on us men a long time ago, but don't get it twisted, love. The men you considered men were nothing more than boys," Derrell spoke freely.

"So let's say you were correct. How the fuck does that help me?" Caria replied. Derrell placed his lips on hers and pulled her body deep into his as he hugged her in his arms tight to remind her that she was all woman and that she didn't need the tough armor around him before he let go. Caria's face was bloodred from embarrassment for being branded like a woman and liking every minute of it.

"We can discuss the rest of that conversation if we make it through this alive," Derrell said as he chuckled.

"Derrell, I know my reasons for helping Felicia, but why are you helping her? I mean you just hired her and she's a complete stranger to you, right?"

"Yes, she is, but there is something about her that I just can't shake. She's innocent and fiery at the same time. She makes you want to get involved with her, from her mysterious eyes to her beautiful inviting smile. Her body makes you come for her. She's everything a stranger wants to know. I'm sure you understand what I mean. After all you were the first one who got the chance to indulge in her sweet fantasy," Derrell replied still smiling at her.

Derrell could tell Caria was getting jealous from the way he spoke of Felicia, but he didn't care. He wanted them both, and nothing was going to get in the way of him having them.

"You could just get us out the way now," Caria responded.

"No, thanks. It's either the both of you at the same time or nothing at all," Derrell replied.

"Well, you know she has a husband, Derrell!"

"Yeah, I know, but that didn't stop you now, did it? I'm just going to put this out there. I'm not interested in jealousy; and if that's what you call yourself being, you can leave now because I need clearheaded people, not clouded and stained with uncertainty,"

Derrell replied as he continued typing on his devices, and then a buzz rang through.

"*Yes.*"

"Sir, there's a Ron here."

"Great, show him the way in please," Derrell replied to the soft voice. "When he gets down here, I'm going to let you two have my office, and both of you need to figure out a way to make this work. Or you're all going to die because enemies can't work well together!"

"Wait, Derrell. How the hell do I do that? This man can't stand my fucking guts, and you want me to go in a closed office with this fool. *Are you fucking nuts*?! *Do you want me to die*?!" Caria shouted.

"You're a grown ass woman, and the last time I checked, you added *independent* on it. So take your grown independent ass on. I'm sure you will come up with something to resolve this issue. And, Caria, you have less than twenty seconds to figure it out, love. Enjoy"

To Be Continued

CPSIA information can be obtained
at www.ICGtesting.com
Printed in the USA
LVHW050436230520
656338LV00006B/782

9 781640 969520